RETURN OF THE JEDI

BEWARE THE POWER OF THE DARK SIDE!

AN ORIGINAL RETELLING OF *STAR WARS: RETURN OF THE JEDI*

BY *NEW YORK TIMES* BEST-SELLING AUTHOR

TOM ANGLEBERGER

P R E S S

Los Angeles • New York

© & TM 2015 Lucasfilm Ltd.

All rights reserved. Published by Disney • Lucasfilm Press, an imprint of Disney
Book Group. No part of this book may be reproduced or transmitted in any form or
by any means, electronic or mechanical, including photocopying, recording, or by
any information storage and retrieval system, without written permission from the
publisher. For information address Disney • Lucasfilm Press,

1101 Flower Street, Glendale, California 91201.

Printed in the United States of America

First Edition, September 2015

1 3 5 7 9 10 8 6 4 2

V381-8386-5-15219

ISBN 978-1-4847-0913-9

Library of Congress Control Number on file

Reinforced binding

Interior art by Ralph McQuarrie and Joe Johnston

Cover art by Khoa Ho

Design by Pamela Palacio and Jason Wojtowicz

Visit the official *Star Wars* website at: www.starwars.com.

This book is dedicated to the earthbound, but amazing,
members of the 501st and Rebel Legion!

AUTHOR'S NOTE

GO RIGHT AHEAD and skip this and head straight for Jabba's palace with R2 and C-3PO. You can always come back later. . . .

Wow, man . . . Jabba's palace! Incredible! The greatest thing ever! Next to the trench run in *A New Hope* and the AT-AT attack in *The Empire Strikes Back*, and the mynocks and the Imperial Royal Guard, and Nien Nunb and Lando flying the *Falcon*, and Han and Chewie flying the *Falcon*, and Obi-Wan fighting Grievous, and Fives on the run, and every scene with Yoda . . .

There's just so much to love about *Star Wars*. And I wanted to cram as much of it as I could into this book. I wanted to give you a story overflowing with the crazy details: What lives in Jabba's nose? What did Mon Mothma say to Leia? How did the Ewoks kill stormtroopers?

And in fact, the story did overflow into footnotes, which you can also skip if you get in a hurry.

Star Wars is important to me. And I wanted to write a book for other people who feel the same way.

George Lucas and huge teams of incredible people made this great movie back when I was a kid. I saw it and I loved it. I *really* loved it.

And now it's up to me (with help from a small team of incredible people, like my editor, Tomas Palacios) to tell you a story you probably already know.

Not every story is worth reading if you already know the ending.

But *this* story is.

This story is the rebels' *last* hope. It's the treacheries of Jabba and the heroics of the Ewoks. It's Princess Leia zooming through the trees on a speeder bike. It's Yoda's final words of wisdom. It's the Emperor's sick smile. It's *ZAP-ZAP, SCREEESH*, and *KAPOW!* And it's *yub nub* and *beep-whistle* and *WHHHHRRRRRUUUGGG!*

I waited three years to see this story on-screen when I was a kid; then I bought the action figures and trading cards (red set); and then I waited for the video to come out years later. I had a blast retelling it as an adult.

The story is *Star Wars: Return of the Jedi.*

And this is my version. I hope you like it.

TOM ANGLEBERGER

A long time ago in a galaxy far, far away. . . .

Luke Skywalker has returned to his home planet of Tatooine in an attempt to rescue his friend Han Solo from the clutches of the vile gangster Jabba the Hutt.

Little does Luke know that the GALACTIC EMPIRE has secretly begun construction on a new armored space station even more powerful than the first dreaded Death Star.

When completed, this ultimate weapon will spell certain doom for the small band of rebels struggling to restore freedom to the galaxy. . . .

JABBA'S
PALACE

CHAPTER ONE

✦

IN WHICH TWO ROBOTS PLOD THROUGH AN ENDLESS DESERT

AN ENDLESS DESERT.

Two robots.

Two robots plodding through an endless desert.

Fear not, reader! It will get better!

But not every story can start with a bang. Or a wampa attack, for that matter.

It's where the story is going that counts, and we've got a big bang coming and an even bigger bang after that and a whole lot of medium-sized explosions, implosions, fireballs, crashes, smashes, lightsaber battles, and evil dark lightning in between.

You may know all about those already. If so, you

know that your patience will be well rewarded once we get through this endless desert.

So, we plod on!

Two robots . . . an endless desert . . . plod, plod, plod . . .

Yes, it really is an endless desert. It fills this whole planet. You might wander around forever and see nothing but sand . . . that is, until someone—or something—pops out from behind a dune and eats you.

But our brave heroes plod on and on under the scorching heat of Tatooine's twin suns. They are droids. Sort of like robots, but better.

One is golden and tall, walking on legs like a man. The other is white and short, with three legs, a bunch of tiny, retractable arms, and a silver dome that spins around so that he can keep an eye on things.

Together they have had many adventures and faced many dangers and now they plod on through this deadly desert without fear or complaint.

Well, perhaps a few complaints.

"We'll never make it Artoo," says the tall one, C-3PO.* "Sand is already accumulating in my servomotors and my joints are freezing up!"

"*Beeep whirr,*" replies the short one, R2-D2, and although we cannot be sure what this means, it has a reassuring sound to it.

"Almost there?" snaps C-3PO. "How can you say that? You have no idea where we are. We've been wandering for ages."

"*Bleeee blip!*"

"Following the road? What road? This is like no road I've ever seen."

It was a road . . . once. Leading through the Dune Sea to a monastery. Though crumbling and near forgotten in these days of landspeeders and

---

*C-3PO is a protocol droid, a machine designed for light duty in luxurious surroundings. However, he was made on Tatooine many years ago and was specially modified to withstand the planet's sand and heat. His companion, R2-D2, is an astromech droid, designed to withstand just about everything.

suborbital hoppers, the road still leads to the same place, but that place is no longer a monastery.

In fact, it is quite the opposite. It is the unholiest of all places on this unholy planet . . . the monastery is now the lair of intergalactic crime lord Jabba the Hutt.

At last, the droids pass a rocky outcropping and see Jabba's palace in the distance. C-3PO's relief circuits barely get warmed up before his self-protection mode kicks in again.

"We're doomed!"

"Breeep!" Again, a reassuring tone from the small droid.

"Of course, I'm worried," fusses C-3PO.* "And you should be, too. Poor Lando Calrissian never returned from this awful place."

"Whirrr." A less confident tone this time.

---

*C-3PO has, in fact, been known to complain too much. But not this time. This time, in fact, he has underestimated the horrors that lie ahead. R2-D2, who knows much, chooses to say little just now.

"If I told you half the things I've heard about this Jabba the Hutt, you'd probably short-circuit!"

As they enter the shadow of the building, a small creature darts across the road behind them, running fast on its twelve legs. But not fast enough!

That rocky outcropping turns out to be not a rocky outcropping at all, but some sort of desert predator. In an instant, it has cracked open a huge toothy mouth, shot out a long tongue, caught, chomped . . . and gulped down the creature, twelve legs and all.

And now it closes its mouth, settles back into the sand, becomes to all appearances a rocky outcropping again, and waits for its next victim.

And, ahead of our robotic heroes, Jabba is waiting, too.

CHAPTER TWO

✦

IN WHICH WE MEET JABBA

JABBA THE HUTT is a giant, evil space slug. And like a slug, he's rather helpless on his own. Tiny arms, no legs, no armor, no weapons.

Well, he does have one weapon—his mind.

A mind vile and corrupt even by Hutt standards. By the sheer force of his own greed, he has risen to the top—or perhaps the bottom, depending on your point of view.

As the most feared crime lord in the galaxy, he can afford to hire all the help he needs—smugglers, thieves, bounty hunters, and plenty of piglike warriors to guard his palace.

Just as a slug prefers to hide under a rock, Jabba

has chosen a dark, damp place for his palace. The nicer rooms are like a dungeon and the dungeon is . . . unspeakable.

It's a fortress, really. So deep in the dunes that the desert itself is all the defense generally needed. Even so, under Jabba's orders the old monastery was obsessively fortified by master armorers.*

Yes, it's the perfect place for this rancid crime lord to slither away and hide, wallowing in his slimy pleasures and chortling over his ill-gotten treasures.

And his newest treasure—for which he had to pay the cunning bounty hunter Boba Fett a medium-sized fortune—is Han Solo.

Solo is well-known now as a hero of the Rebel Alliance, but not all that long ago he used his mighty spaceship, the *Millennium Falcon*, for smuggling, not freedom fighting.

---

*After presenting Jabba with the bill for their services, these armorers became Jabba's first prisoners and never escaped the thick walls and cruel traps they themselves had devised.

He and his copilot, Chewbacca—the great, hairy Wookiee—ran into some trouble and had to dump their load of "spices." Unfortunately, these quite illegal goods belonged to Jabba, and the crime lord did not take the news well.

Solo, unable to pay back the price of the spice, paid a different sort of price: captured by the heartless bounty hunter Boba Fett, Solo was encased in a block of carbonite—a process that left him alive but frozen in time.

And there he lies—or, rather, hangs—on Jabba's wall. His hands reaching out helplessly, his eyes wide with terror, and his mouth stuck in the same scream of pain, Solo will remain like this forever if Jabba has his way.

And Jabba *always* has his way.

He rather likes looking at Solo's frozen agony. Normally, a victim's suffering is over all too quickly. But this way Jabba can slowly savor Solo's pain.

Safe in his dark hole, the slug can fill his belly with forbidden, still-kicking foods, lick his barely dressed slave dancers, and bask in the worship of his minions, henchmen, servants, and toadies.

And if the wearying work of running a criminal empire ever gets him down, he can turn his terrible orange eyes toward Solo and find new reason to let out one of his stomach-turning giggles.

And when Jabba *really* giggles—really finds something worthy of merriment—even the worst of the criminals who sit at the foot of his throne cower inside.

CHAPTER THREE

✦

IN WHICH THE DROIDS
KNOCK AT JABBA'S DOOR

WHO CAN BLAME C-3PO for hesitating at the door of this fearsome building?

"Artoo . . . are you sure this is the right place?"

"Whrrrr."

"I better knock I suppose."

He lightly raps his thin metal fingers against the monstrous iron gate, so thick that a Gamorrean battle-ax would be needed to knock properly.

"There doesn't seem to be anyone here, Artoo. Let's go back and tell Master Luke."

"TEE CHUTA HHAT YUDD!" screeches a barking metallic voice.

This is not, of course, the voice of R2.

It is instead coming from a speaker attached to an electronic eyeball on the end of a long mechanical arm, which has just popped out of a small hatchway in the door.

The eyeball glares quite rudely at C-3PO.

"Goodness gracious me!" exclaims C-3PO. Then, recalling his programming as a protocol

droid and master of six million languages, he intro-
duces himself.

"*Seethreepiowha bo Artoo Detwoowha.*" He points to R2
and the eyeball snakes over to have a look. "*Ey toota
odd mischka Jabba du Hutt.*"

Now the eyeball whips back to focus on C-3PO
again. It lets out a grating laugh and zips back into
the hatchway, which slams shut.

"I don't think they're going to let us in, Artoo. We'd better—"

"*Whhrrrr—*" begins R2, but he is interrupted by a terrible screech.

The massive door is slowly rising upward, revealing nothing but blackness ahead.

R2 looks at C-3PO. C-3PO looks at R2. And R2 rolls ahead into the gloom.

"Artoo, wait!" pleads C-3PO. "Artoo, I really don't think we should rush into this!"

But already, somewhere in the walls, the unoiled wheels and gears have reversed and are now closing the great door again.

What choice does C-3PO have? He must rush in, too, or be left out, alone in the endless desert.

So he steps forward into the darkness.

"Oh, Artoo! Artoo, wait for me!" cries C-3PO.

Behind him, the door continues to screech its way down until, with a horrible crash . . . *BOOOOOOMKKKKKRRRRRRT.*

It closes.

CHAPTER FOUR

✦

IN WHICH A PLAN IS REVEALED

TWO DROIDS against a castle full of evil thugs and a giant, even more evil space slug? You might ask: *What foolishness is going on here?*

Well, it *is* rather foolish, but it's not quite as bad as all that. It's actually the two droids, three people, and one Wookiee against the castle full of evil thugs and a giant, even more evil space slug. (To be truthful, there's also a monster in the basement, but more on that later.)

But why do it this way? Why not swoop in with spaceships blasting, laser guns zapping, Wookiees bowcasting, proton torpedoes laying waste to everything in sight?

No, no, no! Remember this is a *rescue* mission.

The problem for Solo's friends was how to get him out of Jabba's lair alive.

With the aid of the rebel fleet, they could have blown the place to bits . . . but that would have destroyed Han Solo as well. Carbonite is tough, but not that tough.

The Rebellion's ground troops could have attacked—but against Jabba's defenses and weapons stockpiles, it would have been a bloody battle, if not a small war.

Besides, the Rebellion's army and fleet are desperately needed for the endless battle against the evil Empire, which even now is plotting anew to crush the Rebellion* and bring a terrible new order to the galaxy.

No . . . though Han Solo had risked his life for the Rebellion, the Rebellion could not risk its life for him.

---

*It's a very good plot to crush the Rebellion, I'm sorry to say. More on this later . . .

So it was up to his closest friends:

the loyal and hairy Chewbacca,

the not-always-so-loyal Lando Calrissian,

the farm boy turned star pilot Luke Skywalker,

and the rebel princess Leia Organa

to come up with a better plan.

A very risky, very dangerous, very easy-to-go-wrong, very unlikely-to-work sort of a plan.

The sort of plan that was so unlikely to work, in fact, that C-3PO would never have agreed to be part of it.

So he wasn't told.

And now, as the door slams shut behind him, it's too late to turn back.

CHAPTER FIVE

✷

IN WHICH THE DROIDS ARE
WELCOMED INTO THE PALACE

A S THEIR ELECTRIC EYES instantly adjust to
the darkness, what the droids see is so unset-
tling that even R2 gives a nervous whistle.

Two Gamorreans—the piglike brutes that
guard Jabba's palace—lumber forward. A primitive
race, the Gamorreans never would have found their
way off their home planet by themselves. But once
discovered, they flourished* in any place on any

---

*Though well paid by Jabba for their services, they still live
primitive, simple lives. Nesting together in a filthy pit, they
rarely change their stinking garments or wipe the streaming
mucus from beneath their snouts, but in every free moment they
can be seen polishing their crude armor or sharpening their pre-
posterous battle axes.

planet where muscle is valued above brain and violence above wisdom.

Even brutes such as these get bored and it has been days—a week even?—since they have been called upon to dismember one of Jabba's guests. But now their tiny, tiny eyes glitter with excitement.

These two droids might stir up some sort of trouble. Trouble often leads to dismemberments! So they are quite happy to welcome the droids into the palace, though of course they show their pleasure by growling and needlessly prodding the droids forward.

"Oh, my! Oh! Oh, no!"

C-3PO wants to stir up no trouble. He just wants to leave quickly.

"Just you deliver Master Luke's message and get us out of here!" he tells Artoo. But R2 knows the message isn't for these foul brutes.

Then something worse than a Gamorrean appears. . . .

It's a Twi'lek* named Bib Fortuna, a vile, snake-eyed busybody who believes himself to be Jabba's second-in-command.

"Die Wannga Wanga!" snarls Fortuna in Huttese.

"Oh, my," says C-3PO. *"Die Wanna Wauaga!* We—we bring a message to your master, Jabba the Hutt."

"Beep—re-de-click," adds R2.

"And a gift," translates C-3PO automatically. Then he looks at R2. "A gift? What gift?"

Fortuna also looks at R2 when the word *gift* is mentioned. Perhaps the gift could be for himself, he thinks.

"Nee Jabba no badda. Me chaade su goodie . . ." he murmurs. *The guards needn't hear about this,* he thinks. *Keep it quiet and Jabba needn't hear about it either. . . .*

---

*Now, Twi'leks are not all vile. In fact, some are considered quite pleasing to look at. But just as an evil life can make a man an ugly man, an exceptionally evil life has made this creature an exceptionally ugly Twi'lek—as much a worm as anything else, with teeth and lumps and tentacles protruding from his pasty pale-skinned head in very unpleasant ways.

But then the small droid gets quite noisy, beeping and squawking.

"He says that our instructions are to give it only to Jabba himself," C-3PO explains. Fortuna is displeased to discover that this tall golden droid is not only obnoxious, but also far too loud. The Gamorreans have heard too much already and in fact are crowding in—maybe to make sure Jabba gets his gift or maybe to try to grab a piece of it for themselves. Fortuna doesn't care to find out.

"*Nudd chaa,*" he barks, waving a hand at the droids.

He stomps off toward a low, dark archway, from which comes a noxious odor that the droids luckily cannot smell. But they have enough sensors and chem-receptors to know that they are entering a fetid hole of filth and stink.

"Artoo, I have a bad feeling about this," says C-3PO as the piggish guards push them forward.

CHAPTER SIX

✷

IN WHICH WE MEET JABBA
AND HIS GUESTS

AH, YES, now we come to the point where Jabba simply *must* be described. I tried to avoid this a few chapters ago, but I fear there's just no other way forward.

But we can delay a little bit by describing some of the other creatures found in his throne room.

There are a couple dozen of them. It's early yet and some are still sleeping off a night of grotesque excess.

These are some of the worst creatures from across the galaxy. They're unwelcome on their home planets. There is an ugliness here that goes far beyond the unusual features of the different species—the tentacles, horns, fangs, and claws of Jabba's guests have been put to use and are stained with the blood of innocents.*

I'm sorry to say that the cruel bounty hunter Boba Fett is here, too, and who is stained with more innocent blood than he? In truth, Boba grows bored here. Having captured Han Solo, he is Jabba's favorite now and lives in a sort of luxury, with no pleasure denied to him.

But Boba has never sought pleasure; he seeks only the pain of others. And payment, of course. Boba is always thinking about the payment.

Not all here are evil and ugly, though. Jabba collects beautiful women of many races to keep as playthings—or sometimes as meals. There lies one now, dressed in an uncomfortable, revealing costume and chained to Jabba's throne. She is one of the beautiful Twi'leks—different from Bib Fortuna both in appearance and soul. Betrayed by a jealous

---

*In fact, one of Jabba's bodyguards, the reptilian thug Klaatu, is not only stained in the blood of innocents; his tunic seems to still be wet with it.

rival long ago, her life has slipped further and further down into shame and humiliation. And now she has fallen as far as one can. She is a slave, forced to dance for Jabba's delight.

And next to her is Jabba's pet—a nasty monkey lizard named Salacious Crumb, who is actually quite happy to cavort and cuddle with his master, picking up crumbs and drippings and laughing at the terrible doings in the throne room. Some of those who have come here to seek the favor of the crime lord only pretend to laugh at Jabba's jokes, but not Crumb. His laughter is real. It comes from the heart—a tiny, black, loveless heart.

And now, we must—yes, I'm afraid we must—follow Bib Fortuna through this unwashed throng of villainy as he approaches the greenish-brownish-yellowish blob of bloated fat that is his master: Jabba the Hutt.

I've described him before as a space slug, but even the brain slugs of Nusa Sept V are not quite so bad to look at, for their mouths don't open quite so wide and their tongues don't slither about their faces. And of course, they don't have eyes.

And it's Jabba's eyes that are the *worst*. The tons of fatty flesh, the mucus-dripping nostrils crawling with parasites, the yards of scabby, seeping skin— these are all things you might find on a monster or beast if you went looking in the worst places.

But Jabba's eyes are not the eyes of a monster or a beast. They are sharp and alert, alive with extraordinary intelligence. These are the eyes of a genius: a mind that is clever and cunning even for a Hutt. The eyes of a predator who will outthink, not just overpower, its prey.

And now those eyes focus on C-3PO and R2 . . . and they narrow menacingly when Fortuna mentions the name Skywalker. Jabba has heard of Luke Skywalker before: a moisture farmer from near Tosche Station who got mixed up with Han Solo. In fact, Jabba's been waiting for Luke to show up to try to rescue his friend. This should be some good sport! This should relieve the boredom!

Let the game begin, he thinks. As he leans forward, laughing and drooling, a fresh wave of mucus streams from his nose in anticipation.

CHAPTER SEVEN

❂

IN WHICH JABBA LAUGHS AT LUKE'S MESSAGE OF PEACE

AT THE FOOT OF THE THRONE, C-3PO bows.

"Good morning!"

"*Bo SHUDA!*" chortles Jabba, fat rippling in all directions.

"The message, Artoo, the message," says C-3PO, the hope of a hasty exit still flickering in his circuits.

A beam of light pours from one of the many lenses on R2's dome, splitting the darkness of the throne room and creating a hologram image of Luke Skywalker dressed in black.

The hologram begins to play:

"*Greetings, Exalted One. Allow me to introduce myself. I am Luke Skywalker, Jedi Knight and friend to Captain Solo.*"

Many of the half-slumbering creatures in the

throne room stop their sordid doings to watch. This could get interesting.

"I know that you are powerful, mighty Jabba, and that your anger with Solo must be equally powerful. I seek an audience with Your Greatness to bargain for Solo's life."

Here Jabba laughs. *Yes, yes!* This is exactly the sort of thing he was hoping for.

The various thugs, smugglers, slavers, and general scum in the room laugh, too, mostly because Jabba laughed and it's best to please him. Salacious Crumb, however, laughs with anticipation. He knows that some fun is coming.

Meanwhile, the holo-recording of Luke continues, unaware of this reaction:

"With your wisdom, I'm sure that we can work out an arrangement which will be mutually beneficial and enable us to avoid any unpleasant confrontation."

Alas! Unpleasant confrontations are Jabba's favorite kind!

"As a token of my goodwill, I present to you a gift: these two droids. Both are hardworking and will serve you well."

"What did he say?" says C-3PO with all of his alarm circuits lighting up. "That can't be! Artoo you're playing the *wrong message!*"

But it's far too late for anything like that. The message has been delivered and Jabba spews forth his answer in Huttese.

"Bah! Onowanjee Huuu!"

Even if C-3PO hadn't known the language of the Hutts, Jabba's meaning would have been unmistakable: "There will be no bargain!"

"We're doomed," croaks C-3PO.

"Peecha wanjee kopa. Bah noni ettraki droi SOLO incapitta," continues Jabba merrily, meaning: "I like Captain Solo where he is. I will not give up my favorite decoration."

Jabba waves his arm toward a small alcove and for the first time C-3PO sees what is hanging there.

"Artoo, look! Captain Solo! And he's still frozen in carbonite."

Jabba laughs.

CHAPTER EIGHT

✦

IN WHICH THE DROIDS ARE TAKEN TO THE DUNGEONS

A GAMORREAN GUARD pushes R2 and C-3PO out of the throne room and into the conveniently located dungeons.

"What could possibly have come over Master Luke?" chatters C-3PO. "Is it something I did? He never expressed any unhappiness with my work. Oh! How horrid! *Ohh!*"

A tentacle has reached out from a filthy cell they are passing and wrapped itself around C-3PO's neck.

The Gamorrean pounds it with a big fist. The tentacle jerks back into the cell, releasing C-3PO, who spins and totters awkwardly down the stone corridor after R2-D2. Normally he would have complained at length about this treatment, but a door grinds open and he is faced with fresh horrors.

This is the palace's boiler room where huge, ancient furnaces produce enormous heat, billows of steam, and surprisingly little power.

Over the years this has become the center of operations for Jabba's robotic servants—a combination charging center, workshop, junkyard, and torture chamber.

Even as C-3PO and R2-D2 enter, a machine is slowly ripping the arms and legs off one old cyborg while a hapless gonk droid lies upside down as a torture-bot applies white hot brands to its feet. What could a droid do to deserve such treatment? Falling into Jabba's hands is all it takes, I fear. Nothing more than what C-3PO and R2 have already done.

"Ah, good! New acquisitions," says a voice somehow both mechanical and cruel. It is EV-9D9,* a

---

*Originally a peaceful hardworking moisture evaporator mechanic, she has risen to the top of this junk heap thanks to some very nasty reprogramming in a Mos Eisley scrapyard.

tall, thin robot missing various parts that might have made her look less like a skeleton.

"You are a protocol droid, are you not?" she asks C-3PO.

"I am See-Threepio, human-cyborg relations and—"

"Yes or no will do," snaps 9D9.

"Oh. Well . . . yes. I am fluent in over six million forms of communication and can readily—"

"Splendid! We have been without an interpreter since our master got angry with our last protocol droid and disintegrated him."

"Disintegrated?" groans C-3PO.

EV-9D9 waves a hand at a pile of scrap dumped near the door of a furnace.

"Guard! This protocol droid might be useful. Fit him with a restraining bolt and take him back to His Excellency's main audience chamber."

The only part of this the guard understands is "guard" and "take him back," so he pushes C-3PO back through the gloom to the exit.

"Artoo! Don't leave me! *Ohhh!*"

"Whurrrrr," calls R2. Then he turns back to 9D9 and lets loose an angry barrage of beeps.

"Blee-dee-bleep-blipp-o-bleep-whrrrrr!"

Luckily for R2, 9D9 doesn't understand some of the more insulting parts of this speech, but she does get the point.

"You're a feisty little one, but you'll soon learn some respect. I have need for you on the master's sail barge and I think you'll fill in nicely."

A prolonged electric scream from the overturned gonk droid provides R2 with a needed reminder that for now it is indeed his mission to obey.

CHAPTER NINE

✦

IN WHICH JABBA PROVIDES HIS GUESTS WITH ENTERTAINMENT

SOON C-3PO FINDS himself back in the throne room, perched on the rear edge of Jabba's great slab of a throne, where he can translate for the globular crime lord as needed. At the moment, however, all he can do is stare in disgust at the scene before him.

Jabba, it seems, is in the mood for a party.

Max Rebo—a pudgy blue blob who plays a keyboard with his feet—and his band are blasting out a raucous rhythmic tune.

Meanwhile Sy Snootles—a blue-spotted, bloated amphibian with big red lips on the end of a worm-like proboscis—sings lyrics that are almost as disgusting as she is. A chorus of fallen alien angels

screeches alongside her, while a short, furry beast, Joh Yowza, cavorts about the room repeating some of the worst of the lyrics at the top of his lungs.*

All this, while offensive to good or even medium-good taste, is hardly the worst of it.

_____

*There are many in the room who dream of silencing Yowza with a blaster, but Jabba seems to like him and Jabba's opinion is the only one that matters.

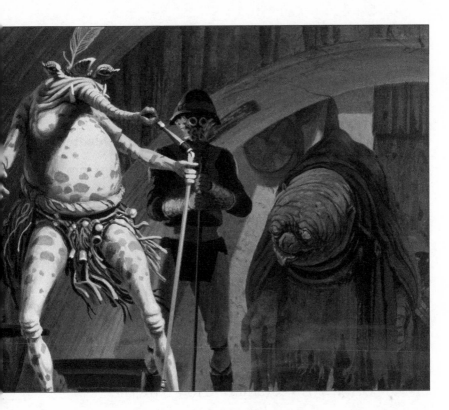

The music is a cue to the dancers that it is time
to shimmy and squirm around in a way that will be
pleasing to Jabba.

Oola, the Twi'lek slave girl, knows how drastic
the punishment will be if she fails to please him.
Though chained to the throne, she dances and
whirls and, alas, pleases Jabba too much.

The great slug pulls the chain with his tiny

arms, desirous of dragging her into his greedy, slimy embrace.

"Da Eitha!"

This is too much. Her revulsion at Jabba's bloated body is greater even than her fear. She flings herself backward.

"Na Chuba negatorie Na!" she begs.

Jabba growls. Pulls harder.

"Na!" she cries. Desperate now she grabs the chain and pulls against him. *"Natoota!"*

"Boscka!" roars Jabba, and now his anger is greater than his desire. This is beneath him! Playing tug-of-war with a Twi'lek dancer! How dare she!

Jabba lets go of the chain to slam his fist down on a button on his armrest.

There is a moment now—a split second—for Oola to realize how dearly she will pay for her refusal to cuddle with the monster.

She hears a clank under her feet and looks down, though she knows what she will see. The floor is falling away underneath her. The button has released a trapdoor.

And now she falls, hitting a rocky floor hard and then tumbling down a short ramp to land in a pit strewn with bones.

She looks up . . . willing to do anything Jabba asks now . . . willing to beg for mercy. . . .

But there is no mercy up there. There is only the crowd of creatures, who have rushed forward to gather around a grating in the floor and peer down into the gloom to watch her fate. They are laughing, cheering, wagering.

Gamorreans rush to push Jabba's throne closer to the grating. And he leans forward to enjoy the show. *This is much better,* he thinks, *much better.*

Oola hears another clank.

At the side of the pit a door is opening. But it is not a way out.

It is a way in. An entrance for another sort of monster.

Where Jabba was weak and bulbous, this one is strong and sharp. All claws and teeth.

What they have in common is greed.

Jabba wants everything, but this monster only wants one thing. Food.

This monster is called a rancor and it is huge and hungry and Oola looks somewhat tastier than whatever it ate the day before and that's about all that's in its tiny brain.

Hungry now! Food here! Eat!

And it does.

In a moment, the party is swinging again. Oola's dying screams haven't dampened the mood at all. In fact, it's quite the opposite. Max Rebo tells the band to kick up the tempo. The remaining dancers shimmy and squirm faster. Salacious Crumb shrieks and cackles.

Yes, everyone is much merrier. . . . Or perhaps they've just been reminded of the penalty for failing to please Jabba.

CHAPTER TEN

✦

IN WHICH MIGHTY
CHEWBACCA IS CHAINED

THE PARTY DRAGS ON. C-3PO wishes he
could leave. More than that he wishes he'd
never come.

And then . . . a shot rings out!

Sounds of a struggle!

A familiar roar! The roar of a Wookiee!

Could Chewbacca be here to save him, wonders
C-3PO, his hope circuits flickering on.

Oh, no! What's this?

Chewbacca in chains?

Yes . . . it is Chewbacca: hero of the Rebellion,
champion of Kashyyyk. A hairy giant, taller than a
man and stronger than ten men. Loyal and true.
Fearless.

He stumbles into the throne room with a bowed head and matted fur, led by a miniscule figure clad entirely in armor. It is Boushh, the famed bounty hunter, known for his lack of height and heart.

"Oh, no! Chewbacca!" yelps C-3PO, his hope circuits flickering out.

Chewbacca gives a low howl but is silenced by the bounty hunter.

Jabba laughs a very nasty laugh.

"At last we have the mighty Chewbacca!" he roars menacingly in Huttese, which is a very good language for roaring menacingly.

The crowd in the throne room can hardly believe their luck. First the thing with the hologram and the robots. Then the slave dancer getting eaten. And now an old enemy for Jabba to play with.

Some edge closer. But some remember Chewbacca from his old days as smuggler and copilot of the *Millennium Falcon* and these keep their distance. Chains or no chains, he is *still* the mighty Chewbacca.

But Chewbacca gives no sign of resistance.

From beneath the bounty hunter's visored helmet comes a strange, scratchy growl.

"Yrrate yraate hru Wookiee."

Jabba waves a hand impatiently and Bib Fortuna raps C-3PO on the head. The droid remembers his new job as translator.

"Oh! Oh, uh, yes, Your Worshipfulness, I am here. He says he has come for the bounty on the Wookiee."

Fortuna hits him again. *"Inna Hutta!"*

"What? Oh dear, well, yes . . ." says C-3PO, and he repeats the line, this time in Huttese.

Jabba slobbers out a reply and C-3PO speaks: "The illustrious Jabba bids you welcome and will gladly pay you the reward of twenty-five thousand!"

Boushh croaks out another line and C-3PO immediately translates.

"Fifty thousand. No less."

Even though C-3PO forgot to translate that bit into Huttese, Jabba knows the meaning well enough and is not pleased!

"Yer wah!"

In his rage, he knocks C-3PO off the throne. Bib Fortuna and a couple of Jawas push him back up.

"What? What did I say?" the battered droid asks as he tries to regain his balance.

"Wonna kitto hrrwhy?"

"Uh, the mighty Jabba asks why he must pay fifty thousand."

Boushh growls out a reply and raises a small silver ball. He slides a finger across it and it begins to glow and hum.

"Because he's holding a thermal detonator!"* cries C-3PO.

The awful noise of chattering aliens and scheming villains has finally been silenced. Each creature is trying to calculate the blast radius and chances of escape. (Zero.) And now only the growing hum of the detonator is heard.

Until the sound is broken by an ugly laugh. It is

---

*A thermal detonator is a clever choice for a situation like this. Not only is it a surprisingly powerful bomb for its size, but it can only be turned off by whoever turned it on.

Jabba and for once none of his toadies laugh with him. Not even Crumb.

"This bounty hunter is my kind of scum," he chuckles in Huttese. "Fearless and inventive. Thirty-five."

"Jabba offers you the sum of thirty-five and I do suggest you take it," bargains C-3PO.

Now everyone watches Boushh. What his thoughts are behind that mask no one can tell. But after a dreadful pause, he slides his finger back across the silver ball and it turns off.

"*Zeebuss*," he mutters.

"He agrees!" yells C-3PO in relief, and even the most hardened criminals in the room cheer with relief. All but Boba Fett, who nods to Boushh with nothing more than professional courtesy.

As for Jabba, he's rather pleased. He would have paid the twenty-five thousand, but now he has no intention of paying the little bounty hunter anything at all.

He's not sure exactly how he'll dispose of the

scheming little cretin, but he'll be sure that everyone sees it. No one threatens Jabba! The bounty hunter will pay and Jabba expects to enjoy it. Contentedly, he reaches into a bowl on his armrest and pulls out a struggling, kicking snack to munch on.

The party starts back up with renewed vigor. Bib Fortuna waves and two guards step forward to drag the miserable Chewbacca away.

Oh, this is a sad sight! How could—

Wait! One of those guards is just another piggy Gamorrean, but the other has handsome features hidden behind a mask made of pit boar teeth.

Incredibly handsome features!

It's Lando Calrissian! True, it was his betrayal that allowed Boba Fett to capture Han Solo.* But since then he has sworn to free his old friend and

---

*And, reader, I must caution you against judging Lando too harshly even for that betrayal. For, though he did put our heroes in jeopardy, he did so to save an entire city from the crushing grip of Darth Vader.

has worked tirelessly to set this rescue plan into motion.

Chewbacca gives Lando a quick growl of recognition and lets the Gamorrean lead him deeper into the dungeon.

Oh, yes, the rescue plan is still in the works. You didn't think Chewbacca would really give up so easily, did you?

Lando watches him go and thinks for a minute about the plan . . . and the risks. But he's a gambler at heart and doesn't dwell on the risks. And anyway, there's no backing out now.

CHAPTER ELEVEN

✦

IN WHICH HAN SOLO WAKES

NIGHTTIME IN JABBA'S PALACE.
Boushh, the bounty hunter, sneaks through the dark. With his visor's night vision, he is able to weave amongst the debris of the day's revelries: castoff dishes smeared with revolting Huttese foods and goblets crusted with the dregs of spice wine, which is illegal even in such a lawless place as Tatooine. But of course there is no law except Jabba's law here in the palace.

What could Boushh be up to? Surely he is not planning to burgle?

Why, yes, it looks like he is! And he has passed up all sorts of ill-gotten booty and made straight for

Jabba's favorite treasure: the carbonite block that is Han Solo.

Quickly, Boushh presses a series of buttons on the control panel. Clearly, the bounty hunter has prepared for this. In a moment he has started the melting process.

The carbon block begins to glow, then emits a harsh blast of light. The carbonite casing is melting away. Han is no longer a statue but appears exactly as he did when frozen by Darth Vader back on Cloud City. But only for an instant . . . then he tumbles forward. Boushh tries to catch him and ease him to the floor.

Han, weak as a baby, lies there coughing and struggling for breath. Boushh cradles him, an oddly gentle move for a black-hearted bounty hunter.

"Just relax for a moment. You're free of the carbonite . . ." murmurs Boushh in his half-mechanical rasping voice.

Already beginning to regain some control of his muscles, Han rubs at his face and moans.

"Shhh!" urges Boushh, again with a puzzling gentleness. "You have hibernation sickness."*

"I can't see," mutters Han.

"Your eyesight will return in time."

"Where am I?"

"Jabba's palace."

If he was well, Han would have leapt to his feet, ready to lunge for an exit. But in his current condition, all he can do is shudder.

"Who are you?" he asks.

Boushh pulls at his helmet. Surely this is hardly the time for him to reveal his grotesque face!

Wait! It's not grotesque at all. In fact, it's not really Boushh.

It's the beautiful Princess Leia, here to rescue Han!

"Someone who loves you . . ." she whispers.

---

*Before the invention of the hyperdrive, some space travelers used carbonite to endure long voyages. But the side effects are brutal. Since a common side effect was death, Solo is lucky to have only exhaustion, weakness, dehydration, dizziness, memory loss, and blindness.

"Leia!"

They kiss, but Leia reluctantly draws away. She is anxious to be free of this place. Lando is waiting for her signal to release Chewie from the dungeon and soon they'll all meet Luke at the rendezvous point and be gone from the palace, then the planet, and then this whole wretched star system.

"I gotta get you out of here," she tells Han, pulling him upright. He can barely walk, but in a moment Chewie and Lando will be able to help. She just needs to get him out of—

"Hwawhhh hwawh hwahhh hwa!" A nauseating chuckle fills the room.

"What's that?" says Han. "I know that laugh."

Leia knows it, too. And she knows what it means. Even as her heart fills with dread, she has the wits to touch a control on her armor. A silent message goes out to Lando and Luke: "Caught!"

A curtain falls open across the room. There, jammed into a small alcove, are Jabba and his most favored cronies. Cramped, sweaty, and slimy, they've waited an hour to spring their trap. And now they are well rewarded.

Jabba laughs again and this time they all join in—slobbery mouths agape, drool and mucus oozing, black hearts rejoicing that it is Han and not themselves that Jabba is playing with.

"Hey, Jabba!" calls Han, trying to summon up the commanding swagger that once allowed him to face the Hutt crime lord without fear. "Look, Jabba, I was just on my way to pay you back, but I got a little sidetracked. It's not my fault."

"Ah cheek a gogh. Yu nee, Solo."

There's no need for C-3PO to translate. There will be no mercy. No bargains. It's too late for any of that.

The money, in fact, means nothing to Jabba. Even the evil pleasure he takes in hurting others isn't what matters here. Solo was a smuggler who lost what he was smuggling. Though he promised to pay Jabba back, he skipped off to join the Rebellion.

The Rebellion means nothing to Jabba. What

matters is that Han made him look weak. Jabba will not let that happen again!

"You may have been a good smuggler once," he chortles in Huttese. "But now you're bantha fodder."

Salacious Crumb cackles with glee, the rest of the throne room laughs, and Jabba roars at his guards to take the smuggler away.

CHAPTER TWELVE

✦

IN WHICH LEIA IS ENSLAVED

"**J**ABBA!" CRIES HAN as he is pulled backward, any hope of swagger now abandoned. "I'll pay you triple! You're throwing away a fortune here."

But Jabba knows exactly what Han is worth. This princess, however, is an unexpected bonus!*

"*Co slayats my!*" he commands: "Bring her to me!"

Lando, who had pushed his way past several Gamorreans to be next to Leia, had hoped to lead her away to the dungeon, then help her escape. But now he has no choice but to lead her forward,

---

*Tipped off by Boba Fett, Jabba had known it wasn't really Boushh under the helmet. But he had guessed that the imposter was just another lowlife smuggler. A short lowlife smuggler. But to his hideous delight it turned out to be a beautiful woman—just a human, but beautiful nonetheless.

toward the one thing in the palace worse than the dungeons: Jabba himself.

"Hwaah hwaah ha," the great slug chuckles greedily.

"We have powerful friends!" snarls Leia. "You're going to regret this!"

Jabba has no need for a translator. He has heard it all before . . . so many times before.

"Ah nah mah toe tah!" he says, licking his lips.

She recoils from his touch, but he draws her closer and closer. She tries to face him, to show him her strength, to stare him down as she once did the Grand Moff Tarkin and, yes, even Darth Vader. But here, within centimeters of his horrible gaping mouth and pimpled tongue, she just can't.

"Ugh!" She turns away in disgust.

CHAPTER THIRTEEN

✦

IN WHICH OLD FRIENDS
REUNITE AT LAST

BELOW . . . IN THE DUNGEONS . . . Han is half
carried, half thrown into a cell. He still can't
see, but the brutal slam of a metal door tells
him that there will be no escape.

And now . . . *"WRGGGGRRRRR!"*

What new horror is this?

But wait: Han knows that growl.

"Chewie?" he calls. "Is that you?"

And just like that, the two old partners are
reunited in a wild, hairy hug that lifts Han off the
ground.

"NGHWWWWWWRGGHHH!"

"Ah, Chewie," says Han as the Wookiee lowers

him to the ground and begins petting and pawing at him.

"Wait! What are you doing in here, pal? What's going on?"

"Ghrrrrnnawug! Mrrrrrrrropf wug Ghrrrrrr!"

"Lando? That double-crossing—"

"HRRKK!"

"What? He's on our side now? I'll believe it when I see it."

"Hrrk wrahhr! Whrrrk!"

"Okay, okay, maybe he is. But how is he going to get you, me, and Leia out of here by himself?"

"Krrrrrrghhhhnn."

"A plan?" repeats Han. "This is a plan?"

"Krrrg Ghrrwph grrr."

"Luke? Luke's crazy! He can't take care of himself, much less rescue anybody!"

The last time Han had seen Luke, he'd had to save the reckless rebel from freezing to death in the snowfields of Hoth. And that wasn't the first time he'd had to save the kid either.

"Nrggh! Jrgghhka wrghhhh."

"A—a Jedi Knight?" scoffs Han. "I'm out of it for a little while and everybody gets delusions of grandeur!"

"Wrrrgggghhhhh!" argues Chewie. But he relents, realizing that Han doesn't yet know about Luke's visit to Master Yoda and his training in the old ways of the Jedi warriors.

"Whrugg!"

"I'm all right, pal. I'm all right."

LUKE SKYWALKER, JEDI KNIGHT

CHAPTER FOURTEEN

❂

IN WHICH LUKE ENTERS
OUR STORY AT LAST

AND WHAT ABOUT LUKE? Where is he?

He is on his way.

Impatiently waiting in the desert cave they chose as a rendezvous point, he leaps to his feet when he gets Leia's message.

Hoping to go undetected for as long as possible, he makes his way through the dunes on foot. He wears a hooded robe, as his first teacher, Obi-Wan Kenobi, wore.

Luke has been thinking much about Obi-Wan lately.

He never expected—and certainly never wanted—to come back here, to Tatooine, his home planet. But once Han's rescue brought him here he felt drawn back—not to his own home*—but to Obi-Wan's.

There, in his master's lonely hermit hut deep in the Juntland wastes, he found a few things Obi-Wan had left behind that were useful to him . . . including the missing parts he needed for the construction of his own lightsaber—the weapon of a true Jedi Knight.

Luke had begun his adventures with a lightsaber that had belonged to his father, Anakin Skywalker.

At first Luke had treasured it. With help from first Obi-Wan and then Yoda, he had learned to use it well and come to depend upon it, to reach for it first when facing any danger.

He had even faced Darth Vader with it, believing that Vader was the man who had killed his father. That was what Obi-Wan had told him.

---

* Luke's own home—where he had lived with his aunt and uncle, who had raised him—had been destroyed by the Empire years ago. In fact, it was that act of evil that had motivated Luke to give up his boring life as a moisture farmer and begin his adventures with Obi-Wan.

But Darth Vader had told him something different. Something darker. Vader claimed that he *was* Luke's father. That he *was* Anakin Skywalker.

At the time, Luke had been sure this was a lie, but he had grown less and less sure. And now he feared that it was the truth.

Whether that lightsaber had belonged to a hero or a villain or both, it was gone now. Lost, along with Luke's right hand, in that devastating battle with Vader on Cloud City.*

To face Vader again, he knew he'd need his own lightsaber.

Luke's teachers, Obi-Wan and Yoda, had told him only a little of the way a Jedi must use the Force to build a lightsaber.

And yet he seemed to know exactly what he needed to know. Reaching out with his mind, he found the right pieces—some easily purchased, some much harder to acquire.

---

*Where Luke had tried—and failed—to rescue Han once before.

After leaving Obi-Wan's hut, he knew he had at last collected everything he needed. While our other heroes bustled about preparing for the rescue, Luke retreated into the solitude of a desert cave and puzzled over the pieces. . . . In the end it took not just physical tools but also the Force to put it all together and bring the crystal inside to life.

But when at last he was finished, a brilliant green beam sprang out—buzzing with a raw, dangerous energy. It truly was his lightsaber, almost an extension of himself.

It pleased him and he grew confident, perhaps foolishly, that if he faced Vader again, the new lightsaber would help him win the fight. But . . . if what Vader had said was true, did he wish to win a fight against his *own* father?

His feelings became confused again. He needed answers. He needed to return to Yoda.

But first, to free his friend Han Solo from Jabba.

So, with this mad plan concocted, he strides through the desert, ready to play his part.

CHAPTER FIFTEEN

───────────── ✦ ─────────────

IN WHICH LUKE CONFRONTS JABBA

NOT EVERY SITUATION calls for a weapon, though, and Luke does not carry the lightsaber as he approaches Jabba's palace.

Perhaps, mindful of the lessons he learned from Yoda, he has decided to seek a peaceful solution and thus brings no weapon at all.

Or perhaps he fears that Jabba would attempt to take the weapon away before letting him speak.

Alas, our hero's mind is not always quite as clear as a Jedi's mind should be on such matters.

Regardless, he is now at the door of Jabba's palace with no weapon, no invitation, no way in, and . . . no certain way out.

The way in turns out to be easy enough. An

electronic eyeball barely has time to pop out before Luke has said, "You will open the door."

Yes, this is a Jedi mind trick and it works easily. Inside, the simpleminded guard who operates the door unthinkingly obeys.

The sudden grumbling and squawking of the opening door awakens the Gamorreans on guard just inside, but Luke doesn't even need to speak to them. A simple wave of his hand and they, too, think letting Luke in is a great idea.

Ah, and now Bib Fortuna scuttles out of the throne room to block Luke's path.

"Yo macka chipowan, Skywalker!"

Here is a better test of Luke's ability. Fortuna is not as simpleminded as the rest.

"I must speak with Jabba," Luke says calmly.

"Es tusi," Bib replies, shaking his head. *"Jabba no tusen di hunka bi. No barga."*

"You will take me to Jabba now," commands Luke and with a small wave of his hand uses the

Force to impress that command on Fortuna's mind.

"*Utaka Jabba nah*," repeats Bib hesitantly.

Luke finds that fooling Fortuna takes consider-
ably more concentration than fooling the guards.
But he quickly perceives Fortuna's weaknesses and
changes his tone.

"You serve your master well," says Luke. "And
you will be rewarded."

This is what Fortuna wants to believe. And, with
the aid of the Force, he does believe it. He turns
and leads Luke toward the throne room, muttering
to himself about his anticipated reward.

Jabba, like many of his guests, is dozing. It was a
late night, what with all that Han Solo business and
the party that followed.

"Master," Fortuna insists. "Master!"

"*Splurp?*" mutters Jabba, half awake.

Fortuna whispers in his ear, "*Gabba nopez Luke
Skywalker, Jedi Knight.*"

"Hah na for waha tooki!" roars Jabba, now wide awake and furious! The one instruction he had given Fortuna was "Don't let Skywalker in until after my nap!"

"I must be allowed to speak," says Luke as calmly as he can.

"Heah mots beyego eek," repeats Fortuna in Huttese.

Jabba whacks Fortuna with one of his tiny arms and attempts to shove him off the platform.

"Koiya baya scoy," he snarls. *"He tosen ano* Jedi mind trick."

"He says you are a weak-minded fool," translates C-3PO. "He says Master Luke is using an old Jedi mind trick."

Fortuna bares his fangs and hisses at C-3PO, but the droid's happiness circuits have taken over.

"Master Luke! At last you've come to rescue me!"

Luke, well used to ignoring C-3PO's chatter, continues staring directly at Jabba . . . but it is not easy to stay focused because Leia is there, too:

miserable and helpless in a skimpy metal dancer's costume and chained to Jabba's throne.

Luke's feelings for Leia are also confused. He knows that he loves her, but in a different way than Han Solo loves her. There's a deep connection, not to mention respect and admiration for her bravery and dedication to the rebel cause.

But now . . . to see her like this . . . a slave, forced to expose so much of herself before Jabba's greedy eyes . . .

Anger wells up in Luke. Hatred, too. Yes, what a pleasure it would be to unleash the power of the Force on this vile creature and be done. It would be so easy. The dark side is calling to him . . . offering him the power to strike down Jabba and anyone else who gets in his way.

Only his Jedi training allows him to control his rage. This is not the time to explode, he tells himself. He must stay focused. After all, there is still a chance to get everyone out safely and peacefully.

He tries to let go of his feelings, as Obi-Wan and Yoda taught him. He tries to focus on overpowering Jabba's mind.

"You will bring Captain Solo and the Wookiee to me," he tells Jabba.

"Ho ho ho ho ho," Jabba laughs, then spits out a few sentences in Huttese.

"He says your mind powers will not work on him, Master Luke," says C-3PO. "He says that he was killing Jedi when being a Jedi meant something. Oh, dear."

"Tell him I am taking Captain Solo and his friends," replies Luke. "Tell him he can either profit by this . . . or be destroyed."

C-3PO translates as requested, but Jabba only laughs.

"It's your choice, Jabba," Luke replies. "But I warn you not to underestimate my powers!"

Jabba clearly understands some of this, because his laugh only becomes crueler.

"Oon bak chi wah, Jedi!"

"He says there will be no bargain and that he will enjoy watching you die," translates C-3PO, adding: "Master Luke, you're standing on—"

But Luke isn't listening. Jabba's mockery has been too much. The anger and hatred and, yes, fear have become too much for him to control. Forgetting his training, forgetting his plan, he uses the Force to reach out for a guard's gun.

It springs into his hand—the grip in his palm, the trigger under his finger. He aims at Jabba and—

He is too late. Jabba has already flipped his switch and the floor has dropped away.

"*BoscSKA!*" he cries gleefully!

Falling, Luke pulls the trigger but misses. He and a hapless guard who was also standing on the trapdoor are tumbling down the hole and into the pit.

The same pit that poor Oola the dancer fell into just yesterday . . .

CHAPTER SIXTEEN

✦

IN WHICH THE RANCOR FEEDS

LUKE IS STUNNED BY THE FALL, ashamed of his failure, and unsure where he is. There is so much in his head that for a moment he doesn't act.

The Gamorrean who fell with him, however, has a single thought in his head: the rancor is coming!

As fast as his bulky body can carry him, the guard tries to scramble up the ramp. It's hopeless and if his brain could hold a second thought, he would know it.

Just yesterday this guard watched the great beast eat Oola. And he cheered it on.

Now he hears his own comrades cheering it on again. He oinks and squeals for mercy, but it's not coming.

Only the *rancor* is coming.

The great iron door rumbles open again.

Crung–crung–crung–crung–crung . . .

Luke doesn't know what's behind it, but he knows he will be fighting for his life. He calms himself. Focuses. A moment ago, a lack of focus led him to make a terrible mistake and use his powers thoughtlessly.

Now he must use the Jedi lessons of his masters to use his powers wisely, to put away fear and anger, to use the Force as a true Jedi would.

"Oh, no! The rancor!" he hears C-3PO cry out from above.

And now the great door is open and the beast is in the pit with them.

The Gamorrean squeals even louder, thrashes about even more violently.

But Luke can now see the rancor with clear eyes. The beast is a horror—one of the nastiest preda-tors from one of the nastiest planets in the galaxy, captured and brought here at great expense—but Luke is not horrified. He studies it intently.

The talons come first. Four on each hand and each one large enough to go right through a man. Though the beast walks slowly on short legs, its long arms and fingers allow the rancor to grab up anything within six meters and stuff it into a gaping, slobbering mouth. It only has fangs. It has no need to chew up plants, only to slice into raw, living meat.

And now, seeing the fat green guard, it does just that. With one last squeal, the guard is chomped in half and swallowed, armor and all. The rancor will cough those up later along with the bones . . . but now it has other business. Another morsel of food is here and the rancor is still hungry.

And now it turns to Luke and he is forced into action, leaping aside just before the claws can close on him. The arms are surprisingly quick, Luke realizes, so he won't be able to dodge them for long. He must go on the attack.

As he leaps to the top of an unsteady pile of rubble, he sees the leg bone of a huge beast, probably a bantha. It's no lightsaber but it is a weapon.

He grabs it, but the time spent pulling it free has cost him. The claws snap closed on him and squeeze tight.

He tries to beat at the great, reptilian hand with

the bone, but it's useless: the rancor barely notices.

The rancor raises Luke to its mouth, which slobbers and smacks in anticipation of this second snack.

Luke stares into the gaping maw. It seems impossibly large. He won't even be a mouthful. But could the mouth be a weakness?

He thrusts the bone into the mouth, not as a weapon this time, but as a wedge. One end is planted just behind the lower jaws and the other catches on the roof of the mouth.

The rancor, expecting a soft, juicy bite, finds that it can't even close its mouth. It roars with fury, whipping its massive head from side to side, flailing its arms. Luke is, for a second, forgotten and dropped.

In its panic, the mad beast strikes the wall, causing a small cave-in. Luke scrambles to avoid being buried. Then he darts into the crack in the wall that has just been created.

He hopes for a rest, but he won't get it. The rancor, with the wild power of a frightened beast, snaps the bone between its great jaws.

In an instant, it has shaken off the fear and remembered the hunger. Again, long, taloned fingers reach out for Luke, probing into the crevice where he hides.

But Luke is ready this time. He has found a

large rock in the rubble of the cave-in and now he smashes it down on the rancor's hand. This does no damage, but causes the rancor to hesitate for a second, which is all Luke needs.

Springing past the gore-encrusted claws, he sprints toward the monster then runs between its legs. The rancor grumpily turns to follow him, but for a moment Luke is out of reach.

He has seen that one section of the pit's wall is a great iron gate. Nearby, a panel has a button. Could escape be this easy?

As the rancor charges at him across the pit floor, Luke jabs the button. The gate does indeed open . . . but behind it is a solid rock wall, with a heavy, human-sized door set into it.

He rushes to the door; maybe he can get through. . . . But no, it's locked from the other side! He peers through the door's barred window and sees that it's even worse than he thought. There are two brutish men on the other side and he barely dodges a spear one jabs through the bars at him.

He spins away and now sees that the rancor is upon him again.

Stooping low to get under the iron gate, the beast leaves no room for him to run or even to dodge the claw that now reaches for him.

But beyond it, he sees the utility panel again. If only he could push the button!

Maybe he can. He grabs for something to throw. The closest thing is the skull of a previous victim. So be it.

He grabs the skull and hurls it past the rancor. A perfect shot . . . aided by the Force. Instead of merely pushing the button, it crushes it. The panel short-circuits with a spray of sparks. The mechanism holding up the iron gate lets go. The great weight is released. Tons of steel fall on the rancor's head, slamming it to the ground and crushing its skull. The great beast is dead.

CHAPTER SEVENTEEN

✦

IN WHICH JABBA IS ANGRY

BUT LUKE'S troubles are far from over.

The small door is unbolted and thrown open.

A giant shirtless man rushes in: the rancor keeper. Instead of attacking Luke, however, he runs straight for the rancor.

And as a crowd of guards surrounds Luke, the rancor keeper weeps for his lost pet.

Jabba is not pleased by the loss, either. The rancor cost him a large fortune!*

Plus, it was fun watching it eat enemies.

---

*Purchasing and keeping one of the most dangerous creatures in the galaxy as a pet is very expensive, but Jabba has always seen it as a valid business expense. It sends an important message to everyone from petty thieves to his fellow Hutt crime lords.

That fun will be gone now.

Someone must pay.

"Yon tas Solo chung Wookiee!" Jabba snarls, demanding that Han and Chewbacca be brought to him. They will *all* pay, he swears.

After several minutes of swinish bustle, the Gamorrean guards drag Han and Chewie in from the dungeons and push Luke up the stairs from the rancor pit.

"Han!"

"Luke!"

"Are you all right?" asks Luke, who until now had no idea if Han was dead, alive, or still frozen.

"Fine," says Han, despite being dizzy, blinded, bound, and repeatedly shoved by a stinking, brutish guard. "Together again, huh?"

"Wouldn't miss it," replies Luke, relieved to see that his friend still has his swagger, if nothing else.

"How are we doing?"

"The same as always . . ."

"That bad, huh?" jokes Han. Still blinded from the hibernation, he asks, "Where's Leia?"

"I'm here," she calls, relieved that at least one person can't see her humiliating costume or the fact that Jabba is petting her with a slimy hand.

Luke sees it all, but keeps his feelings in control.

With his mind focused, he can see the situation more clearly this time. Not all of Jabba's guards and minions are as slow-witted as the Gamorreans. There are several Weequay warriors here, nasty brutes with leathery faces like rotted fruit and personalities to match. Luke recognizes Klaatu, who was infamous on Tatooine for his black deeds when Luke was still a boy. And though Luke has never seen J'Quille before, he can instantly see that the furry giant has fought and won many battles.

And there behind Jabba, watching everyone from behind the thin visor of his dented helmet, is Boba Fett.

With Han blinded and Chewie and Leia both in

chains, this is not the time to make another escape attempt.

But . . . will there be another chance? Not according to Jabba, who is barking out a long string of vicious commands.

"Oh, dear!" says C-3PO. "His High Exaltedness, the great Jabba the Hutt, has decreed that you are to be terminated immediately."

"Good, I hate long waits," quips Han, but it is Jabba who laughs.

C-3PO continues. "You will be taken to the Dune Sea and cast into the Pit of Carkoon, the nesting place of the all-powerful Sarlacc."

"Doesn't sound so bad," says Han.

And now Jabba is nearly gleeful as C-3PO comes to the punch line.

"In his belly, you will find a new definition of pain and suffering as you are slowly digested over a thousand years."

"On second thought, let's pass on that, huh?"

Han mutters to Chewie, who shows his agreement with a howl.

But Luke is still defiant.

"You should have bargained, Jabba. This is the last mistake you'll ever make."

Jabba laughs and his evil cackle is echoed first by Salacious Crumb and then everyone in the crowd.

But why is there a small smile on Luke's face as he and his friends are hauled off again to the dungeon? What could he possibly have to smile about?

Think again, reader, of this dangerous game he is playing against Jabba, with Han as the prize.

Jabba assumes the game is won, but Luke sees it differently.

After a few risky moves, he has positioned all of his pieces just where he wants them. When the game began, Han was alone—and frozen—inside Jabba's fortress. Luke knew that many lives might have been lost by attacking the heavily defended castle directly. So he took a different strategy. . . .

And now they are all inside, with no lives lost, ready to begin the game in earnest.

Ah, but be careful, Luke, the cost of losing this game is high, indeed.

And Jabba cheats.

CHAPTER EIGHTEEN

✦

IN WHICH THE PRISONERS ARE
TAKEN TO CERTAIN DOOM

JABBA, OF COURSE, has never been satisfied with the various landspeeders and skyhoppers that the common folk of Tatooine use to get across the treacherous deserts.

To travel in luxury and style, he purchased a massive sail barge—an energy-guzzling monstrosity that carries him and his entourage five or six meters above the hot sand on a cushion of antigravity.

Today the barge is a floating party. The crowd from the throne room—even Max Rebo and the band—lounges about in the barge's dark, fetid hold. Zooming over the Dune Sea toward the Pit of Carkoon, they indulge in the many pleasures their gleeful host has provided. Jabba is not always so generous, so they are making the most of his good mood.

C-3PO is here and is not having a good time. The rocking and swooping of the sail barge make him stagger across the deck and bump into the most ill-mannered and unspeakable creatures.

Bouncing off a particularly hairy Yarkora, he runs into a bartender droid, knocking over its tray full of drinks.

"Oh . . . I'm terribly sorry!" he exclaims and then takes a closer look. "Artoo! What are you doing here?"

"*Bli-diwip!*"

"Well, I can see you're serving drinks, but this place is dangerous," warns C-3PO. "They're going to execute Master Luke and, if we're not careful, us, too!"

"*Whirrr-chup-fip!*"

"Hmmm . . . I wish I had your confidence!"

———

Belowdecks, in a dark and nasty hold, Jabba is in high spirits.

Today it will be great fun to watch his enemies plead for their lives before being dropped into the Sarlacc's gaping mouth. And tomorrow the story of his triumph will spread across the planet . . . and then the galaxy.

Drooling with the pleasure of it all, he gulps down a glassful of thick, green liquid. It's strong stuff and half this much would kill a lesser creature, but it merely intoxicates Jabba.

And now, for pleasure of another kind, he tugs on a chain to bring his slave dancer close enough for a kiss.

But Leia resists. She has been peering through an opening into the blinding light of the desert outside. Her attention is fixed on two smaller vehicles that float alongside the barge. These are the sand skiffs, used to transport cargo across the desert and occasionally prisoners to their doom.

One of these carries her friends: Han, Chewie, and Luke, all wearing iron manacles and guarded by Jabba's fiercest guards. Leia just has time to see that Lando is among these guards before she is pulled away and then shoved toward Jabba by the greasy claw of Bib Fortuna.

"*Ooh mohla ah yarnee.*"

She doesn't understand or care what he says. In a few minutes, it will all be over—one way or another.

On the sand skiff, Han is at last recovering from the hibernation sickness.

"I think my eyes are getting better. Instead of a big dark blur, I see a big light blur."

"There's nothing to see," Luke tells him. "I used to live here, you know."

"You're going to die here, you know," says Han. "Convenient."

"Just stick close to Chewie and Lando. I've taken care of everything."

"Oh . . . great."

At last there is something to see. The ships have

come to an enormous pit between several sand dunes. While the giant barge coasts to a halt, the skiff carrying the prisoners flies out directly above the center of the Great Pit of Carkoon.

Han can't see and Luke knows better than to look, but Lando takes a nervous glance over the side and recoils in horror. The bottom of the pit is nothing but an enormous mouth, lined with hundreds of long teeth.

This is the Sarlacc.

Sensing that food is coming, it begins extending long tentacles, groping in the sand for any living thing that has come too near. Inside the mouth, a cruel beak begins snapping and grinding in excitement.

The leather-faced guard and another even tougher-looking one who might be his brother—or sister?—have selected Luke as the first course and push him toward a plank that has extended from the side of the skiff.

One of the guards—guided by a Jedi mind

trick—decides to remove Luke's handcuffs. The other shoves Luke roughly onto the plank, high above a fate far worse than mere death.

At last he looks down and sees the terrible thing beneath him—its jaws flexing, teeth gnashing—but then he looks up as C-3PO's voice rings out over loudspeakers.

"Victims of the almighty Sarlacc: His Excellency, Jabba the Hutt, hopes that you will die honorably. But should any of you wish to beg for mercy, Jabba will now listen to your pleas."

"Threepio!" bellows Han Solo. "You tell that slimy piece of worm-ridden filth he'll get no such pleasure from us! Right?"

"WWWWNRRRGGGHHHHH!" agrees Chewie.

"Jabba," calls Luke. "This is your last chance. Free us or die!"

CHAPTER NINETEEN

—————— ✦ ——————

IN WHICH LUKE WALKS THE PLANK

N THE BARGE, all have turned to see Jabba's reaction.

He gives a thumbs-down gesture and the fiends roar with laughter, pushing and shoving to get a view of the Jedi's fall.

With all the commotion, it's easy for R2 to speed up the ramp to the top deck. Rolling into position at the railing, he opens a small flap on his dome, then focuses his vision sensor on Luke.

Luke glances at the other skiff, which the guards are joyriding around in circles. Then he glances sideways at Lando, who gives an almost imperceptible nod. He takes a last look at Chewie and Han and wishes he could see Leia.

The game is set now. Has he been overconfident?

Are the odds too high even for a Jedi? And is he really a Jedi now?

All this must be pushed from his mind. He must focus and allow the power of the Force to flow through him.

And then he flicks his hand in a signal to R2. The droid begins making calculations.

Even as Jabba is roaring out the order to push him in, Luke steps off the plank.

A great cheer goes up from the barge, but it doesn't last long. . . .

Luke spins as he falls. He catches the end of the plank with his hands. It bends and then springs him back up.

Meanwhile, back on the sail barge, R2 fires a small metal cylinder into the air.

PIFWOOOOO...

For an instant, the cylinder and Luke are both in the air at the same time. The cylinder in a high, perfectly calculated arc; Luke making an equally perfect flip to land back on the end of the plank.

He opens his hand.

The cylinder drops into it.

It is his lightsaber and even as he's catching it, he's switching it on.

ZZRRRRAAAPPPP!

And now, Jabba, the game really begins.

CHAPTER TWENTY

---------------- ✦ ----------------

IN WHICH ALL IS CHAOS

INSTANTLY, Luke and his deadly green blade are whirling through the air, slicing into the closest guard, the leathery one, sending him tumbling into the pit.

The other guards on the skiff rush forward . . . all except two: the one who is really Lando and the one Lando now has in a chokehold.

Jabba sees it all from his sail barge and bellows with rage!

"AH MAH KUTTA DA BLASTAH!"

He yells curse-filled commands and his underlings scramble to obey.

Lightsaber roaring and slashing, Luke sends another sluggish, rodentlike guard over the edge and into the pit. That one was easy, but now Luke faces the second of the leather-faced guards, a seasoned warrior who is now enraged by the death of his brother. He jabs expertly with a cruel-looking ax, but with the lightning speed of a Jedi, Luke has already stepped aside, spun around, and delivered a fatal lunge with his lightsaber.

The guard crumples to the deck and Luke leaps across the body to his friends. Quickly he begins to remove the chains from Chewbacca, who has been guarding Han but is eager to join the fight.

"Easy, Chewie!"

But now a blast hits the skiff! Jabba's gunners are firing the sail barge's side laser cannon. The second shot hits the tail of the skiff and it rocks so violently that Chewie clutches Han to keep him from spilling over the rail.

Lando, however, does go over the side! But he manages to clutch a cable as he plummets.

"Whoa! Whoa!" he yells, dangling over the pit with hungry tentacles slithering toward him.

Luke's heart sinks. This wasn't part of the plan. It's not going right. These thoughts eat away at his focus.

On the deck of the sail barge, Boba Fett has been trying to decide if it's worth his while to get involved. The risk means nothing to him, but the size of the reward means everything.

If there was time, he'd negotiate a deal with Jabba, but with things happening so fast, he decides to save the day first and strike a bargain later.

Tapping the control module on his armored glove, he activates his rocket pack, making a graceful leap from one skiff to the other.

Luke, distracted by the chaos and busy freeing Han, hasn't seen him come. But just as Boba raises his blaster to take an easy shot, Luke senses the danger and spins around, his whirling lightsaber slicing right through Boba's blaster.

Before either can react, another blast from the barge cannon hits the skiff's deck, sending up a spray of metal shards and flinging Han and Chewie against the rail.

Chewbacca's been hit by the shrapnel and howls in pain.

"Chewie! You okay?" yells Han. "Where is he?"

Luke glances over to see, giving Boba the time he needs to push a button on his other glove. This time a metal cable snakes out, wrapping around Luke and pinning his arms to his side.

But it's been a long time since Boba tangled with a Jedi, and his tricks aren't good enough. Luke is able to bend one wrist enough to use his lightsaber to sever the cable.

Another laser blast hits the skiff. This one knocks Boba Fett to the deck where he lays, seemingly unconscious or even dead.

A bit of luck for our heroes? Not really, since the same blast nearly shakes Lando off the cable and into the pit. His grip is slipping. . . .

"Han! Chewie?" he calls out in desperation.

With Boba and the guards beaten, they should now be able to pull Lando to safety. But here comes the other skiff! And it's full of fresh guards!

This is where fear might take control of a lesser hero.

The Force is strong within Luke, but he must turn away from fear and focus as his masters have taught him.

There is no time for him to think about this. No time to make a decision.

He either is a Jedi or he isn't.

And now he's in the air again.

Leaping an impossible distance high over the Sarlacc.

Landing on the incoming skiff before the guards can react.

Swirling and striking. A blur of motion. His lightsaber whirring and whirling.

He's killed two guards almost before they realize he's on board.

The other guards open fire with their blasters, but Luke blocks each shot with a sweep of his lightsaber and presses the attack.

Now it is the guards who know fear.

They are no match for a Jedi Knight.

Back on the other skiff, Boba Fett* climbs to his feet and fixes his glare on Luke, only a few yards away on the other skiff.

He raises his armored glove yet again and aims it at Luke, who is too busy avoiding blaster fire to sense it this time.

Chewie sees the danger, but he is too hurt to stop Boba.

"GRRWWWWWWWH!" he howls at Han.

"Boba Fett? Boba Fett? Where?"

"WWWGRRH!"

Han, brandishing a deadly electro-spear dropped by one of the guards, steps forward, swinging it wildly.

---

*He's furious at Jabba and his gunners for shooting at the craft while he's on it, but that's a score he plans to settle later.

Many skilled fighters, even Jedi, have tried to fight Boba Fett before. And they've all failed.

Han Solo on his best day wouldn't stand a chance.

Fett is too good. Too careful. Too cunning. He could never be beaten by skill.

But dumb luck? That's where Solo has always excelled.

The electro-spear hits Boba Fett in the back, sending a wallop of electricity into his jet pack. It ignites instantly.

Boba rockets through the air. He grabs uselessly at the short-circuited controls of the rocket. He has just enough time to think of how silly he must look before he slams into the side of the sail barge and then falls, arms flailing, past the skiffs, past Lando, past the tentacles and the teeth . . . and into the belly of the Sarlacc.

"WURGHRRR!" cheers Chewie.

CHAPTER TWENTY-ONE

✦

IN WHICH THE PRINCESS RESCUES THE PRINCESS

ON THE SAIL BARGE, Fett's fate goes unnoticed by Jabba, who is busy being strangled to death by Leia.

The princess is still chained to the monstrous crime lord, but she secretly gathered up enough of the chain to loop around his neck and yank.

With all his guards busy and his toadies looking for the exit, Jabba is left to defend himself. Faced at last with a true threat to his life, he puts up a mighty struggle. His thick hide and mounds and mounds of fat make him hard to kill.

Leia throws all her weight against the chain,

then, bracing her legs against his bloated belly, and begins to pull it slowly tighter and tighter.

Like Luke, Leia is now beyond fear. And even beyond anger. Jabba simply *must* die!

A grim power flows through her. Jabba thought she was a plaything. But he underestimated this princess.

His great orange eyes bulge from their greasy sockets. His scum-coated tongue lolls out of his grimacing mouth. His tiny hands pull pathetically at the chain.

And at last his tail flops wildly as the last of his life is wrung out of him.

Surely we can we take a moment, even as the battle rages outside, to mark the death of this great villain? A crime lord who cheated and robbed, murdered and plundered for decades. A creature whose greed and cunning were so great that even the Jedi Council had to appease him at times. A criminal who took more pleasure from the crime than the ill-gotten rewards.

This great slug has left behind a mucus trail of pain and ruined lives that will not soon be repaired. But at least it ends here, by the hand of a woman he tried to enslave.

Leia has no time to think of all this. Defenseless in her slave dancer's outfit and still chained to Jabba, she is in great danger.

And so is Lando!

Han, leaning recklessly over the edge of the skiff, holds out the deactivated electro-spear for him to grab.

"Lower it!" Lando yells.

"I'm trying," Han yells back.

Closer . . . closer . . . and—

Another blast from the barge's cannon! And this one takes out the anti-grav propellers on one side of the skiff—the same side Lando is dangling from!

Instantly, this half of the skiff falls. The whole deck tilts wildly. Boxes, tools, a dead guard, and almost everything else in the skiff slides over the side—including Han! Only a quick grab by Chewbacca keeps him from tumbling into the pit with the rest.

The violent motion breaks Lando's grip on the cable and he drops to the sand. He'd be safe here, several meters from the Sarlacc's open maw . . . if not for the tentacles already writhing forward to grab him and pull him in.

Han hangs upside down from the side of the damaged skiff. Chewie has a tight grip on his feet and could pull him up . . . but Han isn't ready to give up on his old friend Lando just yet.

"Grab it! Lando, grab it!" he yells stretching out blindly with the spear. At last Lando catches ahold of it, but before Chewbacca can begin to pull them up another blast hits the skiff, rocking it and pulling the spear just out of reach.

On the other skiff, Luke realizes that the barge's cannon must be stopped immediately before it scores a direct hit on one of his friends—or destroys their skiff and sends them all to their doom!

In one sudden movement, he lunges forward, slicing the last of the guards in two and jumping over the edge of the skiff onto the steep, nearly vertical side of the sail barge. At first he slides down the metal surface but soon finds a finger hold, stops his slide, and—again calling on his Jedi training—begins to climb.

A hatch pops open to his right and a barge guard leans out to fire a blaster pistol. But Luke seizes his arm and pulls—dragging the unbalanced guard through the window and to his death in the pit.

At last, Lando has a good grip on the spear.

"Gently now," says Han. "All right. Now easy, easy. Hold tight, Chewie."

But now one of the thrashing tentacles has reached Lando and wraps itself around his ankle.

"It's got me," screams Lando in pain as powerful suckers grip his leg and the tentacle begins to pull.

"Chewie! Chewie! Give me a gun," shouts Han, reaching back to Chewie, who hands him a blaster he pulled from a guard's dead hands earlier.

Han grabs it and aims it at what he thinks looks like a tentacle.

"No, wait!" yells Lando, looking directly into the barrel of the blaster. "I thought you were blind!"

"It's all right. Trust me. Don't move."

"All right," concedes Lando. "But, a little higher. Just a little higher!"

Han raises the pistol slightly, Lando ducks, and—*PEW!*—a direct hit. The tentacle releases Lando, and Chewie immediately begins to haul them back on board.

But the barge cannon is charged and ready to fire again. *One last shot should finish off the skiff,* the gunner thinks, wrapping a scaly claw around the trigger.

He hears a noise, looks up, sees Luke, sees Luke's lightsaber . . . and never has a chance to pull the trigger.

More guards are surging up the ramp, including the reptilian thug Klaatu.

Luke prepares for the battle, then sees a bigger problem. At the other end of the deck is a far larger gun, with several gunners scurrying to get it charged and ready. One blast from this gun will take out the skiff once and for all.

He rushes for it, using his lightsaber to deflect Klaatu's blaster fire and mow down a Gamorrean just before the brute can swing its ax.

Belowdecks, R2 has found Leia. He extends one of his astromech tools and slices through her chains.

"Come on!" she urges. "We've got to get out of here quick!"

She heads for the ramp, but R2 hears C-3PO calling.

"Artoo! Help! Quickly, Artoo!"

R2 speeds to the spot to find Salacious Crumb cheerfully pecking out one of C-3PO's eyes.

"Oooh! You beast! Not my eyes!" cries C-3PO, flailing his golden arms helplessly.

Again, R2 uses the astromech welding tool. There's a quick zap and then a long screaming howl as Crumb launches himself as far away from the little droid as he can get. Hanging from the ceiling he screeches at them in fury. His tiny brain can't quite realize that his doom is upon him.

C-3PO begins to complain about his treatment, but R2 cuts him off with a "Blee-deep!"

"Abandon ship?" questions C-3PO. "I've heard no such order."

"BLEE-DEEEP!" insists R2 and heads up the ramp with C-3PO stumbling along behind, one electronic eyeball dangling from its socket by a wire.

CHAPTER TWENTY-TWO

✪

IN WHICH ALL ENDS WITH A BANG

U P ON DECK, Leia finds Luke fighting off a small cluster of guards, deflecting blaster shots, and waiting for a chance to lunge forward and strike down each enemy in turn.

"Luke!"

"Leia!" he cries, circling toward her. "You got away from Jabba!"

"But he didn't get away from me!"

Klaatu gets her joke and wonders if Jabba could really be in danger. . . . Perhaps he should go back down and protect his master, he thinks. Or perhaps he should see if he can switch sides before it's too late. . . .

BZZZRAP!

It's too late.

Luke's lightsaber has ended the wicked life of Klaatu and with a loud whirr spins past him to deal with a charging Gamorrean.

But this gives the last guard—a tusk-toothed Snivvian who had hung back while his comrades died—a chance to get off a good shot with his blaster.

PffTHEWW!

The laser bolt hits Luke's hand. He feels the impact, but no pain. He looks at it in surprise, then realizes that it's his artificial hand. The polymer skin has been torn away, revealing damaged servo-motors and wires inside.

Luckily, it still works well enough for him to keep his grip on the lightsaber and parry a second blast from the Snivvian guard. This fight is wearing him down . . . and he knows there may be more thugs and ruffians below deck who will want to take a shot, too.*

---

*Even Rebo's band members are known to be armed and danger-ous, especially Sy Snootles.

He can't fight the whole barge-load one by one.

"Get the gun!" he calls to Leia. "The big gun! Point it at the deck."

Leia quickly climbs up to the gunner's platform. It only takes her a second to figure out the workings of the gun. It's not too different from some of the Rebel Alliance's older equipment. She checks the charge level and reaches for the targeting controls. The great gun turns slowly toward the deck of the sail barge.

Nearby, R2 is trying to keep C-3PO moving.

"Artoo, where are we going?"

"Blip-whirr!"

"Oh, no!" cries C-3PO, coming to a sudden halt on the very edge of the deck and looking down at the sand ten meters below.

"Blee-deep!"

"Oh, no! I couldn't possibly jump!"

R2 doesn't argue but simply rams himself into

C-3PO, sending the protocol droid toppling over the edge. Then he rolls forward and tumbles* after C-3PO.

Luke runs to join Leia on the gunner's platform, whirling to dodge or deflect blaster fire as he goes.

Leaping up to the platform, he slices a cable that runs up one of the sail barge's masts. He gets a firm grip on the end of the cable with his uninjured hand, wraps an arm around Leia, kicks the trigger on the big cannon, and jumps.

They swing out over the Sarlacc pit.

KRRRKAKLAPP! FOOM!

Behind them, the cannon's blast rips through the barge, sending up a storm of metal shrapnel and triggering a series of explosions in the fuel cells.

FOOM! FOOM! FOOM!

Luke lets go of the cable and for a moment they

---

*Somewhere, deep in his memory banks, R2 remembers a time when he could have fired his rocket thrusters and abandoned ship gracefully. But they haven't worked in ages and his warranty is long, long expired.

fall forward in a perfectly timed arc to land neatly on the surviving sand skiff. Chewie, Han, and Lando are helping each other clamber over from the barely floating remains of the other skiff.

Behind them the entire barge is now on fire. As the anti-grav propellers fail in succession, it pitches to one side, splits in two, and slowly crashes into the pit.

"Let's go," calls Luke triumphantly. "And don't forget the droids!"

"We're on our way!" yells Lando, stepping over a dead guard to get to the controls.

Moments later he is lowering the skiff's cargo-magnets to pull the droids out of a sand dune.

And then they're away, zooming across the dunes to safety! A final explosion erupts behind them as the sail barge—and a great deal of evil—disappears in a massive fireball.

A GALAXY AT WAR

CHAPTER TWENTY-THREE

※

IN WHICH OUR ATTENTION TURNS TO THE EMPIRE AND ITS NEW DEATH STAR

ALL THAT ACTION on Tatooine may seem like a clear victory for our heroes, but—alas!—it was not.

For while they've been plotting and planning and risking their lives to defeat Jabba, the *real* villains—the Emperor and his Empire of evil—have not been waiting for them to catch up.

Just think of this: if Vader had simply killed Han Solo in Cloud City, then Luke and his friends would have jumped right back into battle . . . and with new determination.

But by handing Han over to Boba Fett and Jabba, Vader created a costly distraction.

Vader didn't quite realize this, but his master, the evil Emperor Palpatine, had foreseen it. It wasn't really necessary to his plans, but it pleased him to think of all the time and effort Luke would waste on Jabba.

Meanwhile, the Emperor has been quite busy.

Several more star systems have been brought under Imperial rule. Various troublesome political leaders have been assassinated. Vast stockpiles of weapons have been manufactured. And a few dark alliances have been made. For the Emperor is not just an emperor, but also a Sith Lord. He has used the dark side to rise to power, crush the Jedi Order, and expand the reach of the Empire far beyond that of the weak Old Republic.

True, he still has the Rebel Alliance to deal with. A paltry few thousand malcontents who dare to stand in the way of his plans to bring order to a whole galaxy!

But they will be dealt with soon enough.

That plan is already in motion. But it isn't moving quite as fast as he had hoped. So he has sent his most trusted servant, Darth Vader, to sort things out. . . .

CHAPTER TWENTY-FOUR

✦

IN WHICH A SWITCH IS FLIPPED

AH, YOU'RE thinking that the flipping of a switch is a tiny, dull action that cannot matter in a galactic war.

Oh, no, the flipping of switches, the tightening of a bolt, even the filing of paperwork can be just as important as the firing of a gun. It is, in fact, these little things that allow the Emperor to rule a whole galaxy without ever stirring from his chair. He never does any of those things. And yet they get done.

Come, let us look at one of these little, tiny evil deeds getting done.

It starts on a Star Destroyer, one of the Empire's tremendous—and terrifying—triangular spaceships.

The great ship has settled into orbit around the forest moon of Endor. From a docking bay in its belly, a small shuttle emerges, spreads its wings, and zips off toward another object in orbit around the moon—a metal mass so large it dwarfs even the Star Destroyer.

It is the Death Star* . . . a hideous combination of space station, antimatter reactor, and all-powerful weapon.

As big as it is, the Death Star is still growing, still under construction. Not quite a whole sphere yet. But growing every day. Just not growing fast enough to please the Emperor.

Inside the Death Star, countless operators oversee countless screens detailing the various operations of the space station. Much of the work

---

*Of course, this is not the same Death Star that obliterated the planet Alderaan with a single shot. Luke and the Rebel Alliance destroyed that . . . to the Emperor's great displeasure. No, this is a new and improved one.

doesn't seem particularly evil: requisitioning the helmets for a certain squadron of stormtroopers to be moved from floor K39 to floor K47, for instance, or receiving a shipment of elevator propulsors.

But don't be fooled. The end purpose of every action is to promote the Emperor's dark desires. And, reader, we well know that Emperor Palpatine has some very, very dark desires.

They're unspeakable. Unthinkable!

Yet when broken down into tiny pieces, they don't seem so bad. So the helmet supervisor supervises the helmets and the elevator installer installs the propulsors.

And somewhere in the bowels of the giant space station, a flight controller receives a message from the incoming shuttle.

"Command station, this is shuttle ST three-twenty-one, code clearance blue. We're starting our approach. Deactivate the security shield."

"The deflector shield will be deactivated when

we have confirmation of your code transmission," replies the flight controller.

He waits for a signal from his screen, then flips the aforementioned switch, which sends another signal down to the forest moon. There, in the midst of a great forest, a generator the size of a small city is producing a shield around the Death Star.

When the signal is received, a sector of the shield cuts off temporarily to make way for the shuttle.

"You are clear to proceed," the controller announces.

"We're starting our approach," replies the shuttle captain.

And now there's a bustle in the control room. The flight controller rushes to tell the duty officer.

"Lord Vader's shuttle has arrived."

The officer turns on his heel and barks at a petty officer.

"Inform the commander that Lord Vader's shuttle has arrived."

"Yes, sir!" And off he goes.

Meanwhile, the flight controller sits back down. His work is done and he soon forgets all about it.

You were right, it wasn't very exciting. Nonetheless, it is in this way that the Emperor's evil schemes become a dark reality.

CHAPTER TWENTY-FIVE

✦

IN WHICH JERJERROD HOPES DARTH VADER WILL LOOK AT SOME PAPERWORK

"**LORD VADER'S** shuttle has arrived, Commander Jerjerrod," the petty officer announces a few moments later.

Moff Jerjerrod nods.

He already knew this, of course. He's been waiting nervously all morning.

Jerjerrod isn't much of a soldier. He's an architect, a builder, a creator*—not a destroyer.

---

*His high grades at the engineering academy got him a job drafting plans for warehouses. His plans for a freight depot on Ord Mantell got him a job designing ships for Corellian Engineering Corporation. His designs for an interstellar trash hauler got him a job with the Empire.

His job is to manage the construction of this . . .
space station.

Jerjerrod prefers to think of it as a space station,
not a "Death Star."

He has told himself many times that it won't

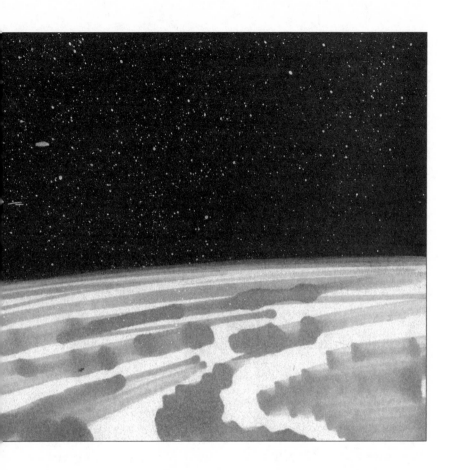

really need to be used. Once built, it will provide a defense for the Empire simply by existing. It will symbolize the Empire's power and deter attacks without ever firing a shot.

Of course, he told himself the same thing when

he helped build the first Death Star . . . which the Empire used to destroy an entire world of innocent people.

But, he tells himself, this time there won't be any need to demonstrate the planet-killing capabilities of this new Death Star.

So day after day he has slaved over plans, sweated over details, exhausted himself with the work of the biggest job in the galaxy.

And it hasn't been easy. Budget cuts! Supply chain breakdowns! And always too many storm-troopers underfoot, yet never enough construction workers to get things done.

He's been asking himself if he will dare to mention all this to Darth Vader. He'd really love to give the Emperor's messenger a long list of complaints and demands.

If only he could get Vader to review the daily reports, to look at the numbers. Perhaps Vader might even take his side! Yes, he *must* show those reports to Vader!

Well . . . probably.

I mean, you know what Vader is like . . . the helmet . . . and the breathing . . . and the soulless black mask.

It's all just a little bit intimidating for an architect turned commander whose only strength is the ability to read those endless reports.

CHAPTER TWENTY-SIX

✦

IN WHICH VADER DOES NOT LOOK AT THE PAPERWORK

ROWS OF STORMTROOPERS stand at attention in the docking bay. They are excited—nervous, even. For most this will be the first time they have seen Darth Vader.

He's far more important than an officer. More than a general or admiral. Certainly more than a Death Star commander, think some, glancing contemptuously at Jerjerrod.

Vader is the right hand of the almighty Emperor. He is the second most powerful man in the galaxy.

And he is terrifying.

He stomps down the ramp from his shuttle with his black cape flying behind him. Even from a distance they can hear the steady wheezing growl of the machinery that keeps him alive, that makes him more than a man.

And even the least Force-sensitive amongst them can feel the power of the dark side as they behold his mask.

He does not just wear the mask. He *is* the mask and the mask is him.

It surrounds his whole head—or whatever is *left* of his head. Instead of a mouth, he has a permanent metal snarl. Instead of a nose, he has a few ugly ridges. And instead of eyes, he has two round black mirrors that reflect the fear of everyone who sees him.

The stormtroopers are safe behind their own masks. No one can see their fear as the deathly gaze of that black mask sweeps over their ranks.

How much worse must it be, then, for Jerjerrod, who has no helmet, no mask, nothing to hide behind? The deathly gaze has landed on him and does not let go.

With swift, tireless strides, Vader is zeroing in

on him. And the horrid mask is really uncomfortably close now. Now it is looming over him! And it's awfully hard to think when that awful mechanical wheezing is filling your ears and all you can see is the reflection of yourself cowering in those awful eyes.

Jerjerrod swallows hard. He wills himself to be strong, but is already abandoning his hopes of showing Vader the reports.

It is all he can do to croak out a formal welcome.

"Lord Vader, this is an unexpected pleasure. We're honored by your presence."

"You may dispense with the pleasantries, Commander," announces Vader. "I'm here to put you back on schedule."

Now Jerjerrod is humiliated in front of the troops. He tries to defend himself.

"I assure you, Lord Vader, my men are working as fast as they can."

"Perhaps I can find new ways to motivate them," booms Vader.

Jerjerrod trembles inside, afraid even to think of Vader's methods of motivation.

This is all going wrong. He takes the strongest stand he can.

"I tell you, this station will be operational as planned."

"The Emperor does not share your optimistic appraisal of the situation."

"But he asks the impossible," says Jerjerrod, his strong stand already becoming a whispery whine. "I need more men."

"Then perhaps you can tell him when he arrives."

"The Emperor's coming here?"

"That is correct, Commander. And he is most displeased with your apparent lack of progress."

"We shall double our efforts," promises Jerjerrod, forgetting all about his list of complaints and demands, all about the reports.

"I hope so, Commander, for your sake. The Emperor is not as forgiving as I am."

And thus we see how Vader gets things done.

How the Emperor runs his Empire.

And how fear makes a not particularly evil architect do the wholly evil deeds demanded by the dark side.

CHAPTER TWENTY-SEVEN

✸

IN WHICH LUKE RETURNS
TO MASTER YODA

FAR AWAY, on the swamp planet of Dagobah, Yoda waits.

For hundreds of years, he taught Jedi younglings the value of patience.

But it has not been easy for him to practice it these last few years.

It is hard to be weak when you were once strong. Hard to move slowly when all around you is moving too fast.

The Force is out of balance. As the Emperor spreads fear across the galaxy, the dark side grows more and more powerful.

Yoda knows that it is Luke's destiny, not his, to

fight back. Yoda—once a warrior, once the leader of all those who stood against the dark side—can do nothing but wait.

And it has been a long, helpless wait. First he waited while Luke went to Bespin, then while Luke rejoined the rebels, then while Luke went on that insanely risky mission to Tatooine.

Using the Force, he has tried to keep watch over Luke, but he has only a sense of what his runaway pupil has been through.

Yet now he senses that Luke is finally returning. And he is relieved. Because he could not have waited much longer.

Already he has used the Force to prolong his life beyond what is natural. Beyond what is comfortable and almost beyond what is endurable. His small body has long ago worn out.

But he refuses to pass on.

Not until he can play his last part in this great galactic struggle.

All he has left are a few pieces of wisdom that might help Luke.

And now, the sound of an engine roars through the swamp, and Yoda knows the time has finally come. The wait is over.

CHAPTER TWENTY-EIGHT

✦

IN WHICH LUKE LEARNS THE TRUTH

"HMMM," SAYS YODA. "That face you make. Look I so old to young eyes?"

"No . . . of course not," says Luke, but of course Yoda does look old. Impossibly old. His green skin is pale and the wrinkles are much deeper than when Luke saw him last. And his long ears are now thin and drooping. And Luke can sense something of the pain inside his old master, though Yoda tries to keep it hidden.

"Sick have I become. Old and weak." But Yoda chuckles. "When nine hundred years old you reach, look as good you will not. Hmmm?"

Yoda hobbles across his tiny hut and climbs onto his bed, struggling even to pull up a blanket.

"Soon will I rest. Yes, forever sleep. Earned it, I have."

"Master Yoda, you can't die," says Luke.

"Strong am I with the Force . . . but not that strong!" Yoda tells him. "Twilight is upon me and soon night must fall. That is the way of things . . . the way of the Force."

"But I need your help. I've come back to complete the training," says Luke, though he already knows he is too late for that.

"No more training do you require," murmurs Yoda, sinking into the bed. "Already know you that which you need."

"Then I am a Jedi," murmurs Luke.

"Ohhh," says Yoda, raising an eyebrow just as he did with hundreds of headstrong impatient younglings over the centuries. But this youngling is different than all of those. If this one fails his final test, then the whole galaxy must suffer.

"One thing remains," Yoda tells him. "Vader.

You must confront Vader. Then, only then, a Jedi will you be. And confront him you will."

"Master Yoda . . . is Darth Vader my father?"

"Mmm . . . rest I need. Yes . . . rest," mutters Yoda, trying to pretend that he didn't hear the question. But he heard it. This is not what he had planned to discuss with Luke. This is dangerous knowledge he had hoped to hide from Luke forever.

But Luke is too close to the truth now.

"Yoda, I must know."

The tired old Jedi rests a moment, gathers his strength, and at last answers Luke's question. "Your father he is."

Both feel this revelation as a blow, as if they had actually been struck by Vader himself.

Luke now knows that his worst fears are the actual truth. He can no longer cling to his hope that Vader was simply lying to him. And with hope gone, fear grows. And so does anger . . . anger that this secret was kept from him for so long.

Yoda never battled Vader face-to-face, but he feels defeated by him at last. Despite all of his efforts and all of Obi-Wan's years of vigilance, Vader has gained a great power over Luke.

His whole life he has sought to banish fear and anger—but now, exhausted and dying, he feels both flicker to life.

Yoda sinks back. Closes his eyes. Seeks to control these dark emotions. After a long pause, he speaks again: "Told you, did he?"

"Yes."

"Unexpected this is, and unfortunate."

"Unfortunate that I know the truth?" snaps Luke.

"No," says Yoda, finding enough strength to turn back to Luke, to face him as a master must face a pupil. "Unfortunate that you rushed to face him . . . that incomplete was your training. Not ready for the burden were you."

"I'm sorry," says Luke.

But he isn't. And Yoda doesn't truly expect him to be.

They both know the reasons for Luke's actions. Luke rushed off to save his friends. He let his feelings come before his duty.

Now, in these last minutes of his long life, Yoda wonders if Luke might have been right. If, perhaps, one's feelings are more important than one's duty.

Perhaps . . . but also more dangerous. So very dangerous. He remembers what happened when Anakin Skywalker put his feelings before his duty—he turned to the dark side, became a tool of the Emperor, and set in motion the destruction of the Jedi.

"Remember, a Jedi's strength flows from the Force. But beware . . . anger, fear, aggression. The dark side are they. Once you start down the dark path, forever will it dominate your destiny."

He draws a painful breath.

"Luke . . . Luke . . . do not . . . do not

underestimate the powers of the Emperor, or suffer your father's fate, you will."

Yes, this was the lesson he had waited so long to teach Luke. And just one more thing. One last thing to tell Luke. One final duty for this Jedi who wanted peace yet spent so many years battling the servants of the dark side.

He has one last thing to say that might help to tip the balance toward the light.

"Luke, when gone am I . . . the last of the Jedi will you be. Luke, the Force runs strong in your family. Pass on what you have learned, Luke. . . . There is . . . another . . . Sky . . . walker. . . ."

And with that he is gone . . . his body vanishes, but Yoda does not quite disappear from the galaxy.

He is part of the Force now, as he always has been and always will be.

CHAPTER TWENTY-NINE

✦

IN WHICH OBI-WAN RETURNS

LUKE IS CERTAINLY NOT in control of his feelings now.

Grief over Yoda's death, confusion over his past and his future, fear of failure, and . . . anger.

Yes, anger. He is angry that Darth Vader is his father. Even though he knew it to be true, he had held out hope that Yoda would explain it all away.

But now it is confirmed. The great dark metal monster who attacked him with such ferocity, such hatred, is his own father.

Of course he is angry, and right now much of that anger is directed at his first master, Obi-Wan Kenobi—Old Ben Kenobi, the crazy hermit from over the dunes who turned out to be a wise and powerful wizard.

Kenobi was the one who set Luke on this path—and he did it with lies.

Kenobi told him that his father was a good man who was killed by Darth Vader. And now Luke knows that was a lie.

So he walks away from Yoda's hut full of all the feelings that Yoda waited so long to warn him about.

There are many dangers in the swamps of Dagobah. Once, when Luke was here training with Yoda, he was alert to every one of them. Even when running at full speed, every step was chosen carefully.

But today he walks carelessly through the muck and mire. There's so much in his head he cannot see what is around him.

He stops briefly to check on some repair work R2 is doing on the X-wing, but he can't focus. He is overwhelmed. Unable to act or even think clearly.

Far away and yet nearby, Obi-Wan senses all this and knows he must help.

Like most Jedi, Obi-Wan became part of the Force when he died.

But Obi-Wan did something the others did not. Guided by the discoveries of his own master, Qui-Gon Jinn, Kenobi found a way to live after death and even return to walk briefly among the living. Not for himself, not for some greedy dream of immortality, but to continue the great fight against evil and tyranny.

It takes a great effort, a great will, but he collects himself, pulls together the pieces of his consciousness from the endless flowing energy of the Force, and appears before Luke.

He cannot do this often, only at the key moments in Luke's journey, when a misstep might spell doom, not only for Luke, but for any hope of bringing balance back to the Force and freedom to the people of the galaxy.

And this, he senses, is the most critical moment of all.

CHAPTER THIRTY

✦

IN WHICH LUKE CONFRONTS
HIS OLD MASTER

LUKE STEPS AWAY from the repair work without ever really seeing it.

"I can't do it, Artoo. I can't go on alone."

And then he hears a familiar voice.

"Yoda will always be with you."

"Obi-Wan!" calls Luke and looks up to see his old master, there but not there, a figure not of flesh and bone, but simply of the Force.

At first relieved, Luke quickly recalls his anger.

"Why didn't you tell me? You told me Vader betrayed and murdered my father!"

Obi-Wan looks away. He understands Luke's feelings, but knows they are dangerous. He must choose his words carefully as he explains himself.

"Your father was seduced by the dark side of the Force. He ceased to be Anakin Skywalker and became Darth Vader. When that happened, the good man who was your father was destroyed. So what I have told you was true . . . from a certain point of view."

" 'A certain point of view,' " protests Luke. He was lied to for his entire life about this one, all-important fact, and now he's told that it was really the truth?

"Luke, you're going to find that many of the truths we cling to depend greatly on our own point of view."

Luke says nothing.

"Anakin was a good friend," Obi-Wan continues. "When I first knew him, your father was already a great pilot. But I was amazed how strongly the Force was with him. I took it upon myself to train him as a Jedi. I thought that I could instruct him just as well as Yoda. I was wrong."

Here Obi-Wan pauses, not wishing to tell Luke

just how wrong he was about Anakin and just how out of control Anakin became, slaying his fellow Jedi—even younglings—and relentlessly trying to slay Obi-Wan himself.

"There is still good in him," says Luke.

Obi-Wan hears this with great pain. Luke is making the same mistake that both he and Yoda made with Anakin, underestimating the dark side's power over him.

"He's more machine now than man. Twisted and evil," says Obi-Wan, again hiding the truth. It was he himself who nearly destroyed the man, leaving just barely enough for the Emperor to rebuild into Darth Vader.

Which truths to tell and which to hide? Sometimes even one as wise as Obi-Wan fails at choosing the right ones. And he feels he is failing Luke now.

Like Yoda, Obi-Wan feels fear—fear that Vader's grip on Luke is already tightening.

"Luke, you must understand. When you face Vader again you must see him as the evil that destroyed your father and so many others. And you must stop him before he destroys yet more. Before he destroys you."

"I can't do it, Ben."

"You cannot escape your destiny. You must face Darth Vader again."

"I can't kill my own father!"

"Then the Emperor has already won," murmurs Obi-Wan. "You were our only hope."

"Yoda spoke of another," suggests Luke.

"The other he spoke of is your twin sister."

"But I have no sister."

"Hmmm. To protect you from the Emperor, you were hidden from your father when you were born. The Emperor knew, as I did, if Anakin were to have any offspring, they would be a threat to him. That is the reason why your sister remains safely anonymous."

But not anonymous to Luke, who finally understands . . .

"Leia! Leia's my sister," says Luke, instantly

recognizing the truth, as if it has never been quite hidden from him at all.

"Your insight serves you well," says Obi-Wan. "Bury your feelings deep down, Luke. They do you credit. But they could be made to serve the Emperor."

Luke looks away, across the swamp into the mist and murk. His mind, however, is clearing.

"What about my mother? Who was she? What happened—"

"No, Luke," says Obi-Wan. "Let that truth stay with me for now. You carry too many burdens already."

Luke starts to argue, but sees the pain in his old master's face and simply nods.

Obi-Wan considers Luke. He cannot see the future as well as Yoda could, but he does sense that Luke will not be able to bury his feelings.

But, just as Yoda did, Obi-Wan wonders if, perhaps, that might not be a failing after all.

Obi-Wan and Yoda and Qui-Gon, too, were

masters of the Force. They buried their feelings and used the Force at its fullest power.

And they failed to stop the Emperor. They didn't even stop Anakin.

Perhaps Luke's feelings really will serve him.

But if not . . . all will be lost.

Obi-Wan can sense his strength growing weak. He cannot bend the laws of nature any further. He must go.

It will be up to Luke now, he realizes. As he fades out of Luke's world and back into the Force, he says the only thing that is left to say.

"Luke, the Force will be with you . . . always."

CHAPTER THIRTY-ONE

---⊛---

IN WHICH THE EMPEROR ARRIVES AT THE DEATH STAR

WHILE LUKE STRUGGLES to find direction, Emperor Palpatine moves with full confidence.

He arrives by shuttle at his new Death Star to find hundreds of stormtroopers lined up to honor him. Think of the resources—the food, the equipment, the money—that it takes to keep so many soldiers on board a space station. And their only job, their only purpose today, is to honor this Dark Lord of the Sith.

And the Dark Lord of the Sith ignores them. They are his tools. He will use them when he needs them, but for now he need not trouble himself about them.

The mastermind behind this epic construction project, Moff Jerjerrod, is there also, bowing before the Emperor.

Palpatine ignores him, too. For weeks, Jerjerrod has exhausted himself and his army of construction workers, driven by the fear of this moment. And now his reward is to be ignored. And Jerjerrod is thankful, very thankful, for this reward. He has not displeased the Emperor and that is enough.

Darth Vader bows, too. And the Emperor does not ignore this. This is the one honor that pleases him. It pleases him to see such a powerful being bow before him.

And, just as Jabba might have tossed a scrap of food to Salacious Crumb, the Emperor treats his apprentice to a tiny morsel of false flattery.

"Rise, my friend."

Vader obeys and follows the Emperor toward the

elevators that will carry them to the just-finished throne room.*

"The Death Star will be completed on schedule," Vader reports.

"You have done well, Lord Vader," replies the Emperor, his voice croaking out from deep within the black hood that hides his hideous face, a face warped by a lifetime of cunning and hatred.

"And now I sense you wish to continue your search for young Skywalker."

"Yes, my master," replies Vader, eager for his master's permission.

"Patience, my friend. In time he will seek you out. And when he does, you must bring him before me. He has grown strong. Only together can we turn him to the dark side of the Force."

---

*See? The elevators are indeed a crucial part of the Imperial war machine. Especially since the Emperor's throne room is located at the top of a tower at the top of the Death Star. Jerjerrod and his workers have had to think of all of this.

This was not the answer Vader had longed for. Patience! For a second a memory sprang up of his days in the Jedi Temple, hearing Yoda preach the same thing. Vader has no more patience, but he does have obedience.

"As you wish," he says with a slight bow.

"Everything is proceeding as I have foreseen."

And here the Emperor laughs.

Jabba's chuckle was hideous, but the Emperor's laugh is far worse. The things that please the Emperor's mind are too terrible to contemplate.

Vader does not laugh with him. Vader never laughs. Has never laughed. Not since he was Anakin. And that is a time he dares not remember.

THE
REBELS
PREPARE
TO STRIKE

CHAPTER THIRTY-TWO

✦

IN WHICH THE REBELLION MAKES BOLD PLANS

O**N THE EDGE OF THE GALAXY,** many parsecs from any Imperial star system, the rebel fleet has gathered near the planet Sullust.

They've given up on maintaining a base on land. This is all that's left, a handful of strange, patched-together starships, a few partial squadrons of fighters, and, of course, the *Millennium Falcon*.

All the pilots have assembled on the flagship to hear from Mon Mothma, the brave leader of the Rebel Alliance.

She's been through so much. She was a weary veteran long before Han and Luke joined up. And now she knows that the long star wars are coming to an end. She plans to commit all of the rebel fleet to one last attack. If they win, they will have cut the head off the great beast and won freedom for her own people and the rest of the galaxy.

But if they lose . . . they will lose everything.

Mothma is not a gambler like Han Solo, though. She is sensible, always sensible. She is taking this course because she believes the rebels can win. But it must be now or never. All or nothing.

"The Emperor has made a critical error and the time for our attack has come," she announces.

The pilots sit up and listen. They had expected another delay or, worse, another retreat. Never this.

Mon Mothma explains: "The data brought to us by the Bothan spies pinpoints the exact location of the Emperor's new battle station. With the Imperial fleet spread throughout the galaxy in a vain effort to engage us, it is relatively unprotected . . . and not yet operational."

Now the pilots are on the edges of their seats.

"Most important of all," continues Mon Mothma, "we've learned that the Emperor himself is personally overseeing the final stages of the construction of this Death Star. Many Bothan spies died to bring us this information."

The Emperor a helpless target on a defenseless space station? It sounds almost too good to be true. Ah, but it won't be that easy. Mon Mothma calls up Admiral Ackbar, veteran of countless starship battles, to explain the details.

"You can see here the Death Star orbiting the forest moon of Endor," says Ackbar as a holographic map of the Endor planetary system appears. "Although the weapon systems on this Death Star are not yet operational, the Death Star does have a strong defense mechanism. It is protected by an energy shield, which is generated from the nearby forest moon of Endor."

Aha, think the pilots, *we knew there was a catch.*

"The shield must be deactivated if any attack is to be attempted. Once the shield is down, our cruisers will create a perimeter while the fighters fly into the Death Star's superstructure and attempt to knock out the main reactor. General Calrissian has volunteered to lead the fighter attack."

Han Solo looks at Lando and raises an eyebrow. He hates to admit it, but he's impressed.

"Good luck," he says, then mutters under his breath, "You're going to need it."

Lando doesn't mention that he's hoping for something more than just luck . . . he's planning to ask Han Solo to borrow his beloved *Millennium Falcon* for the Death Star raid.

But now General Madine is outlining the plan for getting rid of the Death Star's defenses.

"The shield generator is, of course, protected by its own shield. Even if we could get our starfighters close enough, they'd have little chance of knocking it out. However, the moon itself is covered by a thick forest. Perfect for a stealth mission."

"Sounds dangerous," comments C-3PO, unaware that he'll be part of the mission.

Madine continues. "You may have heard that

Nien Nunb recently stole a small Imperial shuttle from an Imperial base."

He gestures to a strange-looking pilot sitting next to Lando. Nien Nunb, one of the few non-human pilots in the Rebel Alliance, beams with pride. There's a murmur of congratulations in the room, but they all know they are not here to celebrate.

"This shuttle has been disguised as a cargo ship," says Madine. "A strike team will fly the shuttle to the forest moon using a secret Imperial code to get past any Star Destroyers patrolling the area. After landing, they will proceed through the forest, locate the shield generator, and destroy it with thermal detonators."

"I wonder who they found to pull that off," Leia murmurs to Han.

"General Solo will lead this prong of the attack," says Madine.

This time it's Lando who raises an eyebrow. This plan sounds risky even for Solo: there are sure to be plenty of Imperial troops guarding the generator.

"Solo, is your strike team assembled?"

"Yes, General," replies Solo.

"HRGGGGRRR!" roars Chewbacca.

"Okay, okay, you can come, too," says Han. "I didn't want to speak for you."

"WRRGHH!"

"Count me in," says Leia.

Han starts to argue but changes his mind. First of all, Leia would be a great addition to the team. And second, he sees the determined look in her eyes and knows she's coming anyway.

"I'm with you, too!"

It's Luke Skywalker, bounding through a doorway to join the briefing. His friends are happy to see him back again so soon, and all the rebels are glad to see the hero of the Battle of Yavin return for such an important mission.

Leia jumps up to welcome him and instantly realizes something has changed since she last saw him.

"Luke, what is it?" she whispers.

"Ask me again later," Luke tells her, both longing to tell her that she is his sister and dreading the other horrible revelation he must deliver: that she is the daughter of Darth Vader.

But he's quickly distracted by the welcome from his other friends, Han, Chewie, Lando, and even his old pilot buddy Wedge.*

Meanwhile, C-3PO has been reunited with R2, who lets out a merry string of beeps.

"Hmmph. *Exciting* is hardly the word I would use," says C-3PO.

---

*Without Wedge, Luke wouldn't have lasted long enough in the Battle of Yavin to be a hero. Now Luke's pleased to see that Wedge has been promoted to squadron leader.

CHAPTER THIRTY-THREE

✦

IN WHICH MON MOTHMA TRIES TO TALK SENSE INTO THE PRINCESS

OUR HEROES seem rather cheerful about rushing off on what their old friend Obi-Wan would have called a damn fool mission.

C-3PO's attitude is far more sensible. But, of course, it was acting sensibly that got the galaxy into this mess in the first place.

Faced with various enemies—The Separatists! Robot armies! Rogue Jedi!—planet after planet had very sensibly allowed the fairly democratic Republic to become the Empire, ruled by the will of a single man.

And by the time some discovered that this sensible man they had chosen was behind the Separatists, the robot armies, and the rogue-est Jedi of them all, Anakin Skywalker, it was all too late and the whole galaxy was made to suffer for a generation.

So we can't blame our heroes for not being sensible.

But for a rebellion to succeed in overthrowing all that the Emperor wrought, some sensibility is required. *Someone* has to make sensible plans. The greatest star pilots still need a working, fueled-up ship to fly in. The bravest commandos need ammo, camo, and a canteen full of water. And if these heroes are successful, then someone needs to be ready to bring order to the resulting chaos.

For the Rebellion, Mon Mothma has been that sensible figure for years. Brave enough to stand up to Palpatine while he was grasping for power and smart enough to know when politics and diplomacy were useless and the time for rebellion had come.

And now she has a tough job to do. She must try to talk some sense into Princess Leia, the daughter of her old friend, Senator Bail Organa.*

You'll recall that Han had considered objecting to Leia coming on the mission. But he didn't dare say so. Mothma, as I've said, is a very brave woman.

"Leia, I know you want to be part of this great adventure with your friends, but the danger is too great."

"You said the same thing about our plans on Tatooine!"

"Yes, and I've since heard how close we came to losing you. Swinging from one ship to another over some sort of sand pit? Really, Leia? Don't you realize how important you are to the Republic we will rebuild someday?"

"But that's exactly what I'm fighting for! What's

---

*Bail Organa was, of course, Leia's adoptive father. Organa, a senator from the planet Alderaan, had always been a trusted ally of the Jedi. So when Padmé died, he and his wife, Queen Breha, agreed to raise Leia and never reveal the secret identity of her real father, Anakin Skywalker. Everyone assumed that she was just another of the many, many children left orphaned by the Clone Wars.

the use of preparing for a Republic that will never exist if *this* mission fails."

"No, Leia, we can't think like that. If this mission fails, then the Rebellion must go on. The rebel fleet, the rebel army . . . they'll be gone. But the rebel spirit will still exist. All across the galaxy. There must be someone to kindle that fire."

"But you . . ."

"Ah, yes, it's always me, Leia. It's always me. I'm always the one that stays behind. . . ."

Mothma turns and looks out the window. The ragtag rebel fleet is swarming with activity. Fuel ships, repair ships, supply ships, troop ships, the medical frigate, and what's left of the starfighters: X-wings, Y-wings, A-wings, B-wings, zipping in and out, up and down . . . preparing for an all-out assault on the new Death Star.

All but one ship. Mothma's ship. It is fueled up and standing by, ready to take her somewhere else, somewhere safe.

"I trained as a fighter pilot once, you know," she

tells Leia. "It was after the Empire's massacre on Kashyyyk.* When I knew diplomacy was dead, I was ready to fight, just like you are now."

This gets Leia's attention. Mothma has always seemed like a friendly old aunt to her, not a fighter pilot.

"Did you . . . ?"

"No. Some people thought I was afraid, and in a way I was. I was afraid of not doing my best for the Rebellion. If I had gone into battle, I might have gotten off a shot, maybe even a lucky shot. I might have helped win the day. But I more likely would have been blasted out of the sky. Something told me I could do much more . . . and I have and I plan to keep on . . . but I can't do it forever. Leia, the new Republic is going to need you just as much as this rebellion does."

"Mothma, I understand. And I will be there for the Republic. But just as something told you to stay

---

*I'd really rather not talk about this if you don't mind. It's too painful.

out of that battle, something tells me to step into this one. I can't explain it. It just feels like it's . . ."

"Your destiny."

"Yes!"

"Yes, I know. And I understand," says Mothma, embracing Leia. "But, for your parents' sake, since they are no longer here to guide you, I felt I had to try to talk you out of it."

CHAPTER THIRTY-FOUR

✦

IN WHICH THE EMPEROR MAKES HIS OWN PLANS

THE EMPEROR has called for his servant, and Darth Vader has come to the Death Star's immense throne room to receive his orders.

To approach the Emperor's throne, visitors must cross a narrow bridge over a vast chasm. If they dare peer over the edge they will see, a mile below, the terrible glow of the space station's main reactor.

Then they must climb several sets of stairs placed there for no reason other than their own inconvenience.

There is no luxury in this throne room. It is all girders and catwalks and strange machinery that hums, buzzes, and sometimes growls.

Even the throne is menacing, more like a chunk of black rock than a chair. It doesn't even have a cushion.

This whole throne room was designed for just one purpose: to intimidate.

And, judging by the way his Imperial advisers* cower together near—but not too near—the throne, it is working. On their own planets, these men walk about like gods. But here, they are humbled.

Vader makes the long climb to the foot of the throne.

"What is thy bidding, my master?" he asks.

"Send the fleet to the far side of Endor. There it will stay until called for," orders Palpatine.

"What of the reports of the rebel fleet massing near Sullust?" asks Vader, eager to be rid of his job babysitting this space station and get back to the real work of the Empire. As soon as he heard about

---

*Although these two men, Sim Aloo and Janus Greejatus, are officially known as advisers, the Emperor uses them more as errand boys. He takes advice from no one.

the whereabouts of the rebel fleet he was ready to lead an attack.

But the Emperor has something different in mind.

"Sullust is of no concern. Soon the Rebellion will be crushed and young Skywalker will be one of us! Your work here is finished, my friend. Go out to the command ship and await my orders."

Vader disagrees and the Emperor knows he disagrees. But he also knows what Vader will say next. . . .

"Yes, my master."

The Emperor has already turned back to his "advisers," leaving Vader to stalk back through the throne room and go forth on his errand.

CHAPTER THIRTY-FIVE

✦

IN WHICH LANDO GETS
THE *FALCON* BACK

THE *MILLENNIUM FALCON* really is a great ship. She started out as just a pretty good ship, but a string of owners modified her to fit their needs. And these needs usually involved being able to outrun and outmaneuver both local and Imperial law enforcement ships.

Lando was one of those former owners and he flew her even better than Han Solo could. Or at least that's what he would tell you.

And now, as he faced the most daring mission of his life, Lando knew he'd need a great ship. And Han would be flying the phony Imperial shuttle. There was no sense in leaving the *Falcon* behind.

After he told all these things to Han a few times, Solo reluctantly agreed.

And now the two old friends stand in the hangar, looking at the *Falcon*, thinking back on all the scrapes and near misses she has been through.

"Look," says Han. "I want you to take her. I mean it. Take her. You need all the help you can get. She's the fastest ship in the fleet."

"All right, old buddy," says Lando, laughing off the danger both to the ship and to himself. "You know, I know what she means to you. I'll take good care of her. She—she won't get a scratch. All right?"

Han knows better than to put trust in Lando's boasting. But after what happened back on Tatooine, he does trust Lando himself.

"Right," he says and turns away. Then turns back. "I got your promise. Not a scratch!"

"Look, would you get going, you old pirate."

They salute each other, as generals should. But they both recall times when their adventures weren't nearly so noble.

"Good luck," says Lando.

"You, too, buddy," says Han and this time he does walk away, to climb into a sluggish stolen shuttle instead of his own ship, to try to bluff his way past an Imperial blockade, to fight his way across an alien moon, and to attack a well-defended Imperial outpost with a handful of soldiers, a Wookiee, a farm boy, a princess, and two droids.

Thinking about it a second, he isn't quite sure why he's bringing along the two droids . . . but, he reasons, they might come in handy.

CHAPTER THIRTY-SIX

✦

IN WHICH THE REBEL PLAN BEGINS

"**B**RING HER OUT of lightspeed, Chewie," says Han, and his furry copilot pulls the lever to disengage the hyperdrive.

The blur of stars and cosmic clouds they've been watching for hours freezes and they are looking at an ominous sight: an immense star cruiser, one of the biggest ships in the galaxy, just ahead.

Beyond it looms something far bigger: the Empire's new space station, the new Death Star.

Jerjerrod still doesn't have it finished and one whole hemisphere trails off into a mess of scaffolding and girders. But even unfinished it still seems unnaturally large.* An insult to the cosmos that has already thrown off the rotation of the nearby moon.

But our heroes are not quite as frightened as

_____

*A dozen planets were stripped bare just to get the raw materials to make this second Death Star. Even now, other worlds are being plundered to obtain the fuel to power it.

they might be. After all . . . they've blown up one of these things before. And this one isn't even work-ing yet.

And yet . . . Leia notices that Luke seems more worried than the rest.

Han and Chewie are busy at the controls.

"Get the nav computer to plot us a course out of

here, Chewie. If they don't go for this, we're going to have to get out of here pretty quick."

"*Yrrrggh,*" agrees Chewie.

But both wonder if this sluggish shuttle could really make the jump to lightspeed before being blown to bits by that star cruiser.

A screen lights up. Incoming message. Han pushes a button and the voice of an Imperial flight controller hisses into the cockpit. A different flight controller this time, but this one has flipped his share of switches, too.

"We have you on our screen now. Please identify."

"Shuttle *Tydirium* requesting deactivation of the deflector shield," says Han, trying his best to sound like a bored Imperial pilot who has done this dozens of times before.

"*Tydirium,* transmit the clearance code for shield passage," comes the authentically bored reply.

"Transmission commencing," says Han, punching the appropriate button.

"Maintain present course until code verification."

Han clicks off the transmit switch and they can do nothing but wait.

"Now we find out if that code is worth the price* we paid," says Leia.

"It'll work. It'll work," promises Han, who, of course, has no way of knowing whether it will or not.

Meanwhile, the shuttle's course carries them closer and closer to the colossal Star Destroyer. *The entire rebel fleet could fit inside it,* thinks Han, and then he remembers that even if he and his team can get the shield down, the rebel fleet is going to have to fight its way past that giant ship to get to the Death Star.

Luke is having even darker thoughts about the Star Destroyer. There's someone on board who's even more dangerous than the countless guns and cannons. Far more dangerous.

"Vader's on that ship," he murmurs.

R2-D2 gives a worried whistle and Leia turns to Luke in alarm.

---

*You didn't think the Bothans worked for free, did you?

"Now don't get jittery, Luke," says Han. "There are a lot of command ships. Keep your distance though, Chewie . . . but don't look like you're trying to keep your distance."

"HHHARGH?"

"I don't know," says Han irritably. "Fly casual."

"Wuggg!"

CHAPTER THIRTY-SEVEN

✦

IN WHICH THE REBELS' TRICK
FAILS . . . YET WORKS

Luke WAS RIGHT, reader; Vader *is* on that ship. He has followed the Emperor's orders and flown out to the Star Destroyer.

Frustrated and restless, he paces back and forth in front of the viewports, accomplishing nothing but scaring the many navigators, flight controllers, petty officers, and other Imperial crewmen.

Admiral Piett, commander of the command ship, really wishes Vader would go elsewhere, but, of course, he will never say so and he even tries not to think so. . . . He has heard rumors that Vader can read minds.

Nothing could be of less interest to Vader than

the admiral's mind. He is barely aware of Piett or any of the crew.

His mind is searching, probing, trying to reach out across the galaxy and find his son. . . .

And then suddenly it does.

And Luke isn't on the other side of the galaxy. He's right here!

Vader turns to the viewport and sees nothing of interest, just another shuttle flitting by. But his mind sees so much more than his eyes. And he knows that Luke is there, on that shuttle.

He turns and in just a few strides is towering over Piett.

"Where is that shuttle going?" he demands.

Piett presses a button and speaks into a comlink. "Shuttle *Tydirium*, what is your cargo and destination?"

"Parts and technical crew for the forest moon," comes the reply.

"Do they have code clearance?" demands Vader.

Piett doesn't know, so he gestures to the flight controller, who always prayed he would never have to speak to Vader.

"It's . . . an older code, sir, but it checks out," he reports. "I—I was about to clear them."

The controller braces himself. He knows what his fate might be if this is the wrong answer.

But Vader gives no response.

The tension has spread to the other flight controllers. Everyone pretends to work, but really just waits to see if their comrade—and maybe even their admiral—is going to die over this seemingly routine shuttle landing.

Finally, Piett can bear it no longer.

"Shall I hold them?" he suggests.

"No," booms Vader. "Leave them to me. I will deal with them myself."

"As you wish, my lord," says Piett. "Carry on, control."

Vader stomps away and everyone on the bridge

relaxes. . . . They have absolutely no idea what got Vader so agitated—and in fact they never will find out—but at least he is gone and they're still breathing.

CHAPTER THIRTY-EIGHT

✦

IN WHICH LUKE REALIZES
HIS MISTAKE

THE IMPERIAL CREW members aren't the only ones who were waiting nervously on Vader's decision.

Back on the shuttle, Han has kept both eyes on the Star Destroyer's cannons, expecting them to swivel in his direction at any second.

What could be taking so long? The code transmission went through several minutes ago!

"They're not going for it, Chewie," mutters Han, putting a hand on the hyperdrive controls.

But then comes a transmission.

"Shuttle *Tydirium*, deactivation of the shield will commence immediately. You may begin your descent, bearing ten dot twenty-two."

"Okay!" says Han, then flicks off the transmitter.

"I told you it was gonna work," he tells his friends. "No problem."

But there is a problem and Luke knows it.

"I'm endangering the mission," he says. "I shouldn't have come. Vader knows."

"It's your imagination, kid," says Han. "Come on. Let's keep a little optimism here."

ENDOR

CHAPTER THIRTY-NINE

✦

IN WHICH WE FINALLY
COME TO A NICE PLACE

AH, THE FOREST MOON OF ENDOR! At last!

Think what it's been like for our heroes. . . .

That endless desert on Tatooine, then the stinking lair of Jabba.

For Luke there was a brief visit to a swamp: all mud and muck, no sunlight.

And the rest of the time has been spent on various rebel spaceships, and let's face it, the rebels can barely keep those things flying. There is no time or money to spend on interior decorating.

And that Imperial shuttle may look nice from the outside, but inside it has been trashed by the countless sweaty stormtroopers it has hauled around. It reeks of stale sweat and every surface is covered in TK numbers* scratched by bored troopers.

So think how wonderful it is for our heroes to tumble out of that junker and breathe in the air of Endor's moon, air purified by a hundred billion trees.

It's hard for residents of developed worlds to wrap their heads around a planet covered in trees.

They may know what a forest is like because they have taken a road or a path through a forest. But at some point, they came out on the other side.

On this moon, the paths (there are no roads) don't come out the other side. There *is* no other side.

There are a few clearings here and there and

---

*Stormtroopers are real people . . . or at least they were once. Before they joined or were forced to join the Empire. Now their identities are stripped away and they are known only by their TK numbers: TK-421, for example.

those clearings are covered in grass. Grass! How long has it been since any of our heroes has seen a blade of grass?

Oh, what a wonderful place, reader! Maybe the best place left in the galaxy. . . .

Which, of course, means the Empire couldn't resist stomping on it with a big ugly boot.

The shield generator could have been built in any of thousands of desolate, lifeless planetary systems. But the Emperor himself picked this spot from several suggested by Imperial engineers.

The engineers liked the idea of burning up the moon's resources to fuel the shield.

And the Emperor liked the idea of crushing something beautiful.

Deep in the official report on the generator site was a mention that the moon was inhabited by a primitive species called Ewoks. It included a hologram of one of these creatures—small, short, hairy with big eyes. They could be a nuisance, warned one engineer.

The Emperor waved the whole species aside impatiently. What does he care about some overgrown rodents? Trod them underfoot and get to work!

Ah, but, Palpatine . . . maybe you should have taken a closer look.

CHAPTER FORTY

✦

IN WHICH IMPERIAL BIKER SCOUTS GET A BREAK FROM THE BOREDOM

VADER COULD HAVE alerted the whole Imperial network to the presence of Luke and his friends on the shuttle.

But he didn't.

He told Admiral Piett that he would handle it personally—and that's exactly what he wanted to do.

However, he failed to mention to Piett that even he—Darth Vader, Dark Lord of the Sith—would need to ask the Emperor for permission first.

So Vader explained nothing. Instead, he sent for his own shuttle to take him back to the Emperor's throne room. Meanwhile, Solo piloted the stolen shuttle down to the forest moon without any further Imperial interference.

At the Imperial base on the moon, an over-worked warehouse manager got a call about an incoming shipment he had never requested. He grumbled about this for a while, but when it never showed up he forgot all about it.

And the Imperial scout troopers patrolling the forest? They didn't get a bit of warning.

Until—way, way out in the woods—one of the scouts hears a twig snap behind him.

He whirls around, expecting to see another of those obnoxious Ewoks. Instead it's a tough-looking human sneaking up on him . . . with a blaster pistol!

This human—who is, of course, Han Solo—looks as surprised by the twig snap as the scout does.

Scout troopers are chosen for their fast reflexes. This one punches Han with a rock-hard, armored glove just as Han pulls the trigger on his blaster.

The shot goes wild, Han goes sprawling, and the scout yells to his partner, "Go for help!"

The other scout jumps on his speeder

bike—basically a gravity-repulsor engine with a seat and handlebars. Long stabilizers on the front allow for precise control even at high speed.

And high speed is exactly what this scout has in mind.

With a flick of the throttle, he's flying through the forest, skimming less than a meter off the ground, and already going incredibly fast.

But not faster than a laser bolt. Chewbacca leaps from behind a tree, levels his powerful bowcaster,* and sends two screaming red blasts after the rapidly disappearing bike.

The scout swoops low to duck the first blast—but the second hits the back of the speeder bike, knocking out the engine. He can't pull out of his swoop, crashes into a fallen tree, and dies in the fiery explosion of the repulsorlift engine.

---

*Bowcasters are more powerful than standard blaster rifles, but are also much heavier. Most humans would have trouble just hauling one around, let alone holding it level and steady for a precise shot. Wookiees don't have that trouble, especially not Chewbacca.

Unfortunately for our heroes, that explosion brings the attention of another pair of scouts. They swoop in to see what is happening.

Most of the rebel strike team is hidden, but the biker scouts see enough to know they're out-numbered. They make a sharp turn—stabilizers shrieking in protest—and head back to the base. The rebels open fire, but the biker scouts are weaving between trees, making a direct hit impossible.

We can't let those two raise the alarm, thinks Leia, racing for the remaining speeder bike. (Han is busy smashing the owner of this bike into a tree.)

"Wait, Leia!" yells Luke, charging after her.

Leia trained on a similar, but much slower, speeder bike on Alderaan. Still, it takes her a few seconds to recognize the controls, giving Luke just enough time to jump on the back of the bike before she stomps the accelerator and shoots off through the forest.

"Hey! Wait!" yells Han.

But Luke and Leia are already half a mile away.

CHAPTER FORTY-ONE

✦

IN WHICH EVERYONE CRASHES

L**EIA IS INTENSE,** dodging living trees, swooping over or under dead ones, struggling to get a glimpse—or even better, a straight shot—at the fleeing biker scouts.

"See if you can jam their comlinks!" yells Luke.

She takes her eyes off the forest for an instant to find the right switch. At this speed that's nearly a fatal decision, but she looks up just in time to swerve around a stump just barely visible amongst the undergrowth.

The switch is flipped just in time, cutting off a transmission from the lead scout to his commander back at base.

The commander—curious, but not particularly alarmed—sends out another pair of biker scouts to investigate. They zip off eagerly. It's probably Ewoks again and that means some fun target practice.

Meanwhile, the two scouts already out there aren't having much fun at all. Leia is actually gaining on them!

Impossible!

Impossible it is not, Luke thinks, remembering the teachings of Master Yoda.

"Move closer!" he yells. "Get alongside that one!"

The scouts swing wide to go around two close trees, but Leia actually shoots between the two massive trunks—so close that Luke feels the bark tear at his sleeves.

The risky move pays off and now they're racing side by side with the second scout. He jerks his handlebars and smashes his bike into theirs. *He's trying to shove us into that tree,* realizes Leia. She splits off just long enough to dodge the tree and then jerks her own handlebars to swerve back, almost knocking the scout off course in return.

The scout swings back to try the same trick

again, but this time Luke is ready and makes a mad leap from the back of one bike to the other.

He lands astride the bike and immediately begins grappling with the scout. As Luke guessed, this trooper is good on a speeder bike, but not much of a fighter. Luke wrenches him off the seat and hurls him off the speeder—just in time for the scout to smash into a tree.

The world stops for this scout, but races on for Luke and Leia. Luke spins out of control for a second, but grabs the controls and pulls up just in time to avoid crashing into a fallen log. He swings back toward Leia and the two share a quick look, then zero in on the remaining scout.

Luke has a shot lined up and is about to pull the trigger when a blast hits his own speeder.

The Imperial reinforcements have arrived! They aren't sure what's going on, but they know Luke and Leia don't belong on those speeders. They open fire again. Several shots miss but one scores, knocking out the landing gear on Leia's speeder.

"Keep on that one!" Luke yells to Leia. "I'll take care of these two!"

He hits the brakes hard, the reverse propulsors make a mighty *whoosh*, and the speeder decelerates so quickly that Luke is almost thrown over the handlebars.

The two scouts behind him zoom past at full speed. Now behind them, Luke crushes the accelerator and squeezes the trigger at the same instant.

Laser blasts shriek through the woods and incinerate one of the speeders. Luke is flying so fast already that he nearly runs into the explosion.

The other speeder drops back a bit now, drawing even with Luke and—*smash!* This scout is playing the bumping game, too, but he's made a terrible mess of it—the front stabilizers of both speeders are tangled!

Neither one can steer and they're headed straight for a tree.

Both men struggle desperately to yank the stabilizers loose and at last they break free—but too late for Luke! He can't dodge the tree!

He throws himself off the speeder bike—

KAKAPOW! "Oof!"

—and crashes to the ground as the speeder explodes overhead.

Luke tears a hole in the undergrowth as his momentum carries him tumbling painfully forward.

Meanwhile the scout makes a long, lazy circle to come back and finish him off, laser cannon blazing as he zeroes in on his slow and helpless target.

BZZRA-pikang! BZZZRA-pikang!

The blazing green blade of Luke's lightsaber easily deflects the blasts! The biker scout has never seen anything like it.

And he gets one last look as Luke steps out of the

path of the speeder, then whirls back to chop off the front stabilizers with his lightsaber.

The speeder and the scout spin wildly out of control and it's now only a matter of which tree they'll smash into.

Ah . . . that one.

Crrrrun-KAPKPOW!

Another fireball in the forest. Let's see . . . that's three fireballs so far. That means there are two bikes left.

Ah, yes, Leia and the lead scout.

It has been a nasty chase and it gets even nastier when the scout pulls a pistol and starts taking sideways shots at Leia.

PZZZEW! PZZZEW!

But these distract him from the forest whizzing past and Leia is sure she can—

PZZZEW!

Too late!

This shot hits her speeder's control panel. The

speeder lurches, throwing her loose and making a nosedive into the base of a tree.

ZZRHHMM-KABLOOSH!

The scout looks back with satisfaction at the particularly large fireball this one made.

Then looks forward again just in time to see the roots of a fallen tree sticking up through the ferns—

KRRRAKKAPOW!

Leia dimly hears the sounds of this fifth fireball as she loses consciousness and slumps to the forest floor.

CHAPTER FORTY-TWO

✦

IN WHICH WE MEET WICKET

WICKET IS A WARRIOR.

Well, a warrior in training. He's not unlike Luke Skywalker, actually, back when Luke was a bored teenager on Tatooine, weary of farmwork and dreaming of big adventure.

Wicket would like an adventure, too.

And he's about to get it.

Wicket is an Ewok . . . one of those rodentlike creatures that live on this forest moon. You remember: the ones Emperor Palpatine dismissed with a wave of his hand.

Wicket is a member of a tribe that lives high in the trees of this forest where Luke and Leia have been chasing scout troopers around on speeder bikes.

Wicket does not like these weird white creatures that fly about with so much noise. They kill Ewoks for sport. Generally when the white fliers are around, the higher you are up your tree the better.

But Wicket has climbed down to the forest floor to check out the place where he saw two white fliers crash. When he arrives, however, he sees a creature that is not a white flier. This creature is not encased in hard white armor, but wears soft green cloth.

And parts of this creature that stick out from under the green cloth look even softer. Wicket sees smooth skin . . . without fur! That is something he has never seen before.

What is this thing? Is it dead? Can you eat it?

He must find out. So he pokes it with his spear.

This is a foolish thing for him to do and he almost dies for his foolishness.

Princess Leia really *is* a warrior, not just a warrior in training.

Prodded by the stick, she wakes up and sees Wicket standing over her.

Immediately her hand jerks for her blaster! Though she's still groggy from the accident, she could draw her gun and shoot a hole through Wicket before he has time to squeal for help.

But she doesn't.

And why not?

Well, if Wicket had been a hideous creature with fangs and claws she would have.

But Wicket is . . . cute. He's tiny—shorter than R2-D2 even. And he's all fuzzy. I mean all over—belly, face, feet, all fuzzy. And he's got a pug nose and two big shiny eyes peering out from under a little hood.

What she doesn't realize is that if *she* had been an ugly creature *he* might have lunged at her with fangs bared and spear stabbing.

But . . . each one has instantly charmed the other. So for a moment they just look at each other there on the forest floor.

Then Leia stands up and Wicket jumps back in alarm. She's enormous!

But she's talking to him in a friendly way.

"I'm not gonna hurt you," she says. Of course he has no idea what the words mean, but he hears nothing threatening, only kindness.

She looks around. It looks the same in every direction: ferns, trees, fallen logs.

With a start she remembers how she got here, the mad chase through the forest and her fall off the speeder. Instinctively, she reaches for her comlink to call Han—then remembers that they agreed that using the comlinks would be a last resort.*

She runs down her options.

She could find the wrecked bike and maybe follow her own trail back to the other rebels. But then again, there are probably more Imperials out there right now following the same trail to find out what happened to all the missing speeder bikes.

Maybe it would be smarter for her to move on toward the rendezvous point. But, she realizes, she

---

*Any electronic communication, even if encrypted, would alert the Empire to their presence.

236

has no idea how to get there. Nor does she know where she is right now, for that matter.

For now she'd better just stay out of sight, she decides. The mission could—and must—proceed without her.

She sits down on a fallen log. And sighs. Is her part in this adventure over already?

"Well, looks like I'm stuck here," she tells Wicket. "Trouble is, I don't know where here is."

And then she realizes that, of course, this little creature probably knows exactly where here is.

"Maybe you can help me," she says.

He growls, but not in an unfriendly way.

"I promise I won't hurt you," she repeats. "Now come here."

She pats the log, inviting him to sit down. Wicket climbs up but doesn't sit. He's curious, but cautious.

Leia has an idea for breaking through the language barrier. She takes a nutri-stick from a pocket and holds it out to him.

"All right. You want something to eat?"

Yes, he does. Ewoks always want something to eat.*

He's never had a nutri-stick before but instantly recognizes it as food. He takes it and finds it very pleasing. An Ewok's diet is usually roots, nuts, and spit-roasted splledarks. Maybe a boar-wolf if the hunting parties have been lucky, or verkles† if the hunting parties have been unlucky.

But this is soft and chewy and—

He jumps back in alarm! The tall creature is taking off its head!

"Mer chee WAYA!" he snarls, waving his spear again. *"Ner esso oohSUM!"*

"Look, it's a hat," Leia assures him. "It's not gonna hurt you. Look." She puts it down on the log and he taps at it with his spear. And then he notices

---

*The Ewok civilization has reached that point where they dabble in religion, medicine, art, even politics, but still focus most of their energies on getting enough food every day.
† Yuck!

that her head is covered with fur. Very long and very beautiful fur.

"Mer bollup bollup," he chatters. And sits down next to her to finish his nutri-stick.

"You're a jittery little thing, aren't you?" she says.

And then suddenly he's up again, spear ready. But this time he's not threatening Leia, he's protecting her.

"Yee so nolla nolla . . ." he whispers.

"What is it?" she whispers back.

KERFZZZZZZZZKRAK!

A laser blast hits the log just next to them.

Instantly, they both fling themselves off the log and crouch behind it.

Blaster ready, Leia risks a peek over the log and—

KERFZZZZKRAK!

Another blaster shot hits the log. And she has no chance to see where it came from. She ducks back down.

Wicket is gone . . . but a biker scout has arrived.

"Freeze!" he barks. Then, "Come on, get up! Give me that blaster!"

Leia considers an attack. She might be able to surprise him: lunge in and knock his gun aside. But she realizes that this scout couldn't have been the one firing the shots. There must be at least one more hidden in the forest with his blaster fixed on her right now.

So she reluctantly hands over her gun.

"She's disarmed," says the scout, and his partner emerges from behind a tree.

"Go get your ride to take her back to base," the first scout says.

"Yes, sir!"

Leia and the first scout stand looking at each other for a moment as the other one stomps back through the ferns.

The scout touches a button on his glove to activate his helmet comlink. "Base? This is—"

But suddenly he is screaming in pain. He looks down to see that Wicket has driven a spear into the gap in his armor at his right knee. The sharp stone tip of the spear is ripping right into his leg.

By the time he remembers to look up again, it is too late. Leia has picked up a branch and is swinging it hard, right at his head. Without his helmet the blow might have killed him. As it is he is knocked out and crumples.

But before he even hits the ground, Leia has snatched the blaster out of his hands.

Leaping up onto the log, she sees the other scout jumping onto his bike.

KERFZAPP! KERFZAPPP! KERFZZZKRAK!

Her third shot hits him and he slumps over the controls. Unfortunately for Leia, his bike now crashes into the other scout's bike and both explode in a double fireball.

KRRRKOOMSHKAKOOMSH!

And then she hears a squeal.

The first scout, though still sprawled on the ground, has revived enough to grab Wicket by the throat.

KERFZZZKRAK!

Leia kills him with his own blaster.

There is a sudden silence in the forest.

Leia and Wicket look at each other with new respect. Each realizes that they have underestimated the other.

And Leia now knows she has an ally she can trust.

"Let's get out of here," she says and the meaning is clear to Wicket.

He sets off through the forest with surprising speed, leading her back to the safety of his treetop village.

Of course, there is no real safety for Wicket or Leia in the treetops of this forest moon. . . .

Not while the great Death Star hangs up there in the sky.

CHAPTER FORTY-THREE

✦

IN WHICH DARTH VADER
IS SENT TO ENDOR

DARTH VADER has been restless ever since he sensed Luke's presence on that shuttle headed for Endor.

That is where he should be. Confronting Luke . . . and, if necessary, erasing that part of his past forever.

But the Emperor has forbidden it. The Emperor has told him to wait.

The waiting is driving him mad.

Each thought of Luke leads to thoughts of Luke's mother, Padmé, the woman he loved and destroyed. And those are thoughts he cannot allow. His Sith powers give him great control over his feelings. It takes constant effort—even after all these years—to keep Anakin's memories buried, but he can do it.

Except not today. Not while he feels Luke so near.

And certainly not while he is forced to wait—unable to block out his feelings with action. If his master would only let him loose he could do so much!

But his orders are to do nothing.

So he stomps back and forth in the Death Star's holding room, waiting for his master to call him. The Emperor calls up various dignitaries, council members, even that fool Jerjerrod. But Vader waits and waits—his own mind driving him closer and closer to madness.

Another of Anakin's memories slips through his defenses: Master Yoda and his constant chant of "Patience, Padawan, patience."

For a moment, his hatred of Yoda gives him relief from those other feelings.

And then, at last, one of the Emperor's annoying red-robed guards motions to him.

Now another wait in the elevator. And now the long walk across the little bridge and up the steps. And at last he stands before the throne.

The Emperor is turned away from him and does not bother to turn around.

So Vader waits yet again.

At last the Emperor speaks.

"I told you to wait on the command ship."

And at last Vader delivers his news. "A small rebel force has penetrated the shield and landed on Endor."

"Yes, I know," hisses the Emperor.

How does the Emperor know? Did one of the biker scouts manage to get a message back to base? Did some flight controller finally realize that there was one shuttle too many? Or does the Emperor simply know these things?

Vader isn't asking any of these questions. His question is, *Then why have I been kept waiting?*

But of course he dares not ask it, hardly dares to

think it. The important thing is that he convince the Emperor to let him go deal with it. To take some action, at last.

"My son is with them," he says.

Finally, the Emperor turns around to look at his servant. Vader's black mask gives away no sign of emotion, of course, but the Emperor can see much deeper than that.

"Are you sure?" he asks.

"I have felt him, my master."

"Strange, that I have not," the Emperor croaks from beneath his hood. "I wonder if your feelings on this matter are clear."

"They are clear, my master."

"Then you must go down to the moon base and wait for him."

More waiting? This is not what he was asking for!

"He will come to me?" asks Vader skeptically.

"I have foreseen it," chortles the Emperor. "His compassion for you will be his undoing. He will come to you and then you will bring him before me. Now go. . . ."

"As you wish," replies Vader with a bow, but the Emperor is already turning away again.

Vader strides back to the elevator, this time with great purpose.

But as he rides down to the docking bay where his shuttle waits, another memory surfaces:

He was a boy on Tatooine. A slave boy. While working in Watto's scrap yard, he found some bit of junk he wanted. A broken servomotor he thought he could repair and use on the droid he was building.

He asked his master, Watto, for it. With a glance, Watto saw that it was worthless, so he grunted, "Yes."

But as Anakin walked away, Watto called, "Nothing's free, boy. I'll work you harder tomorrow."

And he did.

Why did he think of that, he wonders. And why should he be thinking of the past at all?

That was Anakin's past, not his. The past was dead . . . all except that one mistake: his son.

And now at last he was about to correct that mistake by bringing Luke to the dark side. And if he couldn't do that, then he'd erase the mistake entirely.

CHAPTER FORTY-FOUR

✦

IN WHICH OUR HEROES WALK INTO A TRAP WITHIN THE TRAP

LAS, WE KNOW THE TRUTH for certain now . . . this entire mission to the forest moon of Endor is a trap.

The Emperor knows all about the stolen shuttle, the strike team, and the plans to blow up the shield generator.

All the secrecy, all the comlink jamming, all the biker scout chasing—it's all been pointless. The whole thing is pointless.

When Han Solo and his strike team reach the shield generator, they will find a large force of troops waiting for them. They'll be captured or killed and the shield will remain in place. The rebel fleet's attack—and the Rebellion itself—will be equally doomed.

It's all an elaborate trap—foreseen and crafted by the Emperor himself.

But there is a less elaborate trap out there. One that the Emperor has not foreseen.

This trap is made of ropes and vines and baited with a hunk of fresh meat.

It's the smell of this meat* that gets Chewbacca's attention.

He and Han and Luke have separated from the rest of the strike team. For hours they have been trying to find Leia, assisted by R2-D2's sensors and, I'm sorry to say, somewhat hindered by C-3PO's plodding and complaining.

Luke is certain that Leia is still alive—he can sense it. Some time ago they found her helmet near the site of four wrecked speeder bikes and several dead scouts. This made Han sure she was still alive, too.

_____
*Verkle.

Now they are trying to follow her path through the forest undergrowth, but it is slow going, especially with droids—and especially with C-3PO.

"Oh! These vines! I'm hopelessly entangled! You'll have to go on without me, Artoo! The princess is more important than—"

Han and Luke have tuned out his constant complaints and perhaps we should do the same.

Suddenly Chewbacca cocks his head, draws in a deep breath, and runs growling off in a new direction.

"What? Chewie?" calls Han. "What?"

By the time Han catches up with him, the mighty Wookiee has sniffed out the source of the smell, the previously mentioned hunk of fresh meat, dangling from a tree.

"It's just a dead animal, Chewie," says Han, realizing that the Wookiee was after lunch* not Leia.

But, as Chewbacca reaches for the meat, Luke

---

*Apparently, Chewbacca isn't too picky about what he eats.

arrives with the droids and instantly senses the danger.

"No! Wait, Chewie!"

But he's too late—and he wouldn't have been able to stop the hungry Wookiee anyway.

Chewbacca grabs the meat and the trap is sprung.

Again, the trap is not elaborate, but it is clever!

Our heroes never knew they were standing on a large net concealed among the weeds at their feet. When the bait is pulled, a peg is dislodged and high above a bent tree branch is loosed. It springs upward with great force, pulling a rope that lifts the net—and our heroes—into the air.

"*WURRRHHHGG!*" moans Chewbacca.

It is not a dignified scene. A Jedi, a star pilot, a great hairy Wookiee, an astromech, and a protocol droid all squeezed and squashed into the crude net, legs and arms sticking out this way and that.

"Nice work, Chewie!" growls Han. "Just great! Always thinking with your stomach!"

"Will you take it easy?" snaps Luke. "Let's just figure out a way to get out of this thing. Han, can you reach my lightsaber?"

"Yeah, sure," says Han, realizing the lightsaber must be what's been jabbing him painfully in the side. He reaches for it but is too late.

R2 has found another solution. He has extended yet another of his mechanical arms, this one with a small saw blade typically used for cutting through a ship's pipes and cables. It will zip through this homemade rope in no time.

"Artoo," warns C-3PO. "I'm not sure that is such a good idea."

But he's too late. R2's saw cuts through a chunky knot in the net and the whole thing splits open.

The scene becomes even less dignified as our heroes drop to the ground, landing with thuds, groans, and clanks.

Han sits up and quickly notices the tip of a spear being waved in his face. He looks around. More spears.

They are surrounded by a sizable Ewok hunting party.

The Ewoks wave their spears and chatter excitedly. Their trap has worked! They don't know what they've caught, but it does look edible. There will be a feast tonight!

CHAPTER FORTY-FIVE

✦

IN WHICH THE EWOKS MEET A GOD

THESE EWOKS ARE BIGGER and fiercer than
Leia's new friend, Wicket, but compared to
Han or Luke—to say nothing of Chewbacca—
they are still quite small and, yes, cute.

And again, being cute saves their lives here.
If they looked like, say, Greedo, Han and Chewie
would have blasted them to bits by now.

But they just don't seem that threatening. Annoying, maybe, but not a threat.

So instead of reaching for his blaster, Han just
shoves the spear away from his face.

"Point that thing someplace else!"

But the Ewok pushes it back in Han's face. And
another hunter rushes in to join him. Behind them
dozens more cautiously creep forward.

Han frowns. This could turn into a big annoyance and they don't have time for annoyances right now—they've got to find Leia.

Reluctantly, he goes for his blaster, but Luke stops him.

"Han, don't. It'll be all right."

At first it is compassion that makes Luke stop Han. There's been plenty of death already, he thinks, and killing these cute furballs will get them no closer to Leia or the shield generator. And that's when he realizes that these creatures might actually help them find both of those things.

They don't just know the forest like a map. They know it as their home. They are part of it.

Who better to help our heroes through it?

But first they'll have to find a way to make friends with these creatures. . . .

And that's when C-3PO finally recovers from the fall and sits up.

"Oh, my head," he exclaims, then sees the Ewoks. "Oh, my goodness!"

"Ooooooh!" the Ewoks gush, and bow low to the ground.

"Hrrrmgg?" mutters Chewbacca.

"Beats me, Chewie," says Han in amazement.

"Coro way nim-nee ash Knaa Naa?" screeches an Ewok.

"Treetoe doggra. Ee soyoto ambuna nocka," replies C-3PO.

"Eesch shy whise, Moga da eeshrii!" chatters the Ewok in amazement.

"Do you understand anything they're saying?" asks Luke.

"Oh, yes, Master Luke!" chatters C-3PO. "Remember that I am fluent in over six million forms of—"

"What are you telling them?" interrupts Han.

"Hello, I think . . ." replies C-3PO. "I could be mistaken. They're using a very primitive dialect. But I do believe they think I am some sort of god."

Luke and Han can't help but laugh and, of course, Han quickly sees a way to turn the Ewoks' confusion to their advantage.

"Well, why don't you use your divine influence and get us out of this?"

"I beg your pardon, General Solo, but that just wouldn't be proper."

"Proper!"

"It's against my programming to impersonate a deity."

Han, exasperated, reaches over to knock on C-3PO's metal head.

The Ewoks react swiftly, throwing themselves between Han and the droid. Ready to fight to the death to defend their new, golden god.

"Ungat! Hodo unn usk!"

"My mistake," says Han, sinking back down among the ferns with his hands raised. "He's an old friend of mine."

"Yabu shadu abu," growls their leader.

THE
EWOKS

CHAPTER FORTY-SIX

✦

IN WHICH OUR HEROES
ARE REUNITED

SOME HOURS LATER, the Ewoks return triumphantly to their treetop village with much to show off!

First comes the holy C-3PO carried on a wooden throne by about a dozen straining Ewoks.

Then comes the meat: two humans and a Wookiee tied to poles and also carried by about a dozen straining Ewoks each.

And last, another horde of Ewoks carries R2-D2, laid out flat on a sort of wooden raft. For some reason, the Ewoks don't consider R2-D2 at all godlike and have actually tied him up with vines.

This strange parade has the desired effect and

the villagers bow and ooh and chatter in a way that is very pleasing to the hunting party.

And then Han is lowered into position over a barbecue pit.

"I have a really bad feeling about this," says Han, realizing that now he actually *is* rather help-less, with his hands and feet tied to a pole and his blaster confiscated.

Meanwhile, the leaders of the hunting party have been talking excitedly to two older Ewoks. One is the tribe's chief, Chirpa; the other is the shaman, Logray. They all chatter excitedly and Logray waves his stick about mystically.

Chief Chirpa steps forward, one hand on his chief's medallion—a pretty rock—and the other raising his own staff—the leg bone of a great lizard he slew many, many seasons ago.*

"Acha, meecho iyo bugdoo!" he commands.

Several Ewoks rush forward with firewood and

---

*Ah, that was a mighty battle! Remind me to tell you about it someday!

begin arranging it under Han Solo. Others start banging drums.

Han watches all this with growing concern. "What did he say?"

"I'm rather embarrassed, General Solo, but it appears you are to be the main course at a banquet in my honor."

There's a bustle in the doorway of a hut and then everyone looks up as someone much larger than an Ewok ducks through.

"Leia?"

"Leia!"

"*GRHHHHWWRL!*"

"*Wreeeee boo-deep!*"

"Your Royal Highness!"

Yes, it is Leia. She's let her hair down and traded her camouflaged military gear for a dress hastily fashioned from a few of the Ewoks' spare blankets. Somehow, she looks quite at home here in this bizarre village, high in the branches of the forest's mightiest tree.

She rushes forward in confusion, shocked to see Han, Luke, and Chewbacca the prisoners of these tiny creatures.

"What are you doing? These are my friends."

Chirpa waves and several Ewoks with spears step between Leia and the rest.

"Yes, we're her friends," shouts Han. "C-3PO, tell them! We're her friends."

"Roke ta toe-toe," translates C-3PO rather frantically. *"In nee chandu toma tiktik. Ree peetah bah."*

"Ah vey vey vey," insists Chirpa, shaking his head. Then he calls, *"Tohtha ya peek."* An Ewok steps forward with a torch to light the fire pits.

"Somehow I get the feeling that didn't help us very much," moans Han.

"Threepio," commands Luke, "tell them if they don't do as you wish, you'll become angry and use your magic."

"But, Master Luke, what magic? I couldn't possibly—"

"Just tell them."

"*Horomee ana fu, toron togosh! Toron togosh!*" C-3PO warns the Ewoks. "*Terro way. Qee t'woos twotoe ai. Ue wee de dozja. Boom!*"

"*Tohtha ya peek,*" Chirpa repeats, and waves to the torch bearer, who begins to light the wood directly under Han.

"You see, Master Luke, they didn't believe me. Just as I said they wouldn't," says C-3PO, but even before he finishes he begins to rise in the air, wooden throne and all.

"Heeelp! Somebody help! Master Luke! Artoo! Somebody, somebody, help!" yells C-3PO as he begins spinning around and around in the air. "Do something, somebody! Oh! Oh!"

Meanwhile, the Ewoks are terrified, and who can blame them? It's one thing to have a shiny golden god visit your village, but it's another thing to have a shiny golden god floating over your village shouting crazily in an unknown language.

Chirpa barks the orders to free the prisoners, and the Ewoks rush to obey.

Han is freed first and rushes to embrace Leia. Chewbacca is right behind him. R2-D2 is cut loose, tips over with a loud thud, and then pops back up fighting mad. He zaps the leader of the hunting party, Teebo, with one of his astromech tools.

And Luke, quietly concentrating, lowers C-3PO safely to the wooden deck with a small motion of his hand.

"*Oh!* Thank goodness!" the droid exclaims.

"Thanks, Threepio," laughs Luke.

"I didn't know I had it in me," murmurs the droid, quite unsure what has just happened.

CHAPTER FORTY-SEVEN

✦

IN WHICH A FEAST IS HELD
AND A TALE IS TOLD

AH, YES, the Ewoks have their feast. Since the hunters' catch became guests, however, they all have to make do with root stew.

Not quite as bad as Yoda's root stew, though, thinks Luke with a smile.

And then C-3PO begins to tell the Ewoks the story. The whole story!

The story of how he and R2 loyally served the Republic.

FWOOSH! How R2 flew dangerous missions with his rocket thrusters during the Clone Wars.

PZAP! PZAP! PZAP! How the clone troopers betrayed and murdered all the Jedi.

HEH HEH HEH . . . How Chancellor Palpatine became the Emperor and crushed freedom throughout the galaxy.

WSHHHH-WSHHH-WSHHHH. How a Sith Lord in a terrifying black mask appeared to help the Emperor rule through fear and violence.

"Eek!" squeaks Nippett, a small Ewok.

WHOOOOSH! Then brave rebels far away began spreading the word from planet to planet to fight back. And one boy sent a message across the worlds that ignited a spark of rebellion.

THERE'S ONE SET FOR STUN! How Darth Vader and stormtroopers caught one of these rebels, Princess Leia, but not before she had given secret plans to R2.

"Aaah!" said Wicket, beaming proudly at Leia.

PLOD PLOD PLOD! How R2 and C-3PO crashed in the desert and wandered helplessly until they were reunited by the Jawas—*"UTINI!"*—and sold to Luke Skywalker.

DO DO DO DOO DE DOO DEE . . . How they traveled with Obi-Wan Kenobi, hero of the Clone Wars, to Mos Eisley . . .

RGGGGHHAR! Where they met Chewbacca and Han Solo . . .

ZOOOOM! And flew to Alderaan in the *Millennium Falcon*.

"Oh, dear," says C-3PO, pausing his story when he realizes how painful the next part might be for Princess Leia.

"Neeb chub! Neeb chub!" the Ewoks all demand. Leia nods at C-3PO to continue. It is time these Ewoks know the purpose of the Death Star.

So C-3PO goes on, telling the Ewoks how the Empire built a great metal moon that shot fire through the sky and destroyed a whole planet . . . Leia's home planet, Alderaan.

BZAP BZAP BZAP! And then he and R2, along with the others, were held as prisoners on the Death Star, but escaped and very cleverly rescued the princess.

"THIS IS RED FIVE, I'M GOING IN!" And then Luke and R2 flew back to the Death Star in a tiny ship . . .

ZROOOOOSHHHH ZROOOSHHH! And were blasted by Darth Vader and his fleet of TIE fighters . . .

The Ewoks are wide-eyed in terror.

YEEEHA! But Han and Chewie swooped in at the last second and blasted Darth Vader in turn . . .

"Nub chee hoah!" cheers Teebo.

KABLROOOOOOSSSSHHHHHHHHHHHHH! And Luke blew up the Death Star!

Now all the Ewoks are cheering.

"Mirchiwa—"

But their triumphant war cry is cut off by:

WSHHHH-WSHHH-WSHHHH.

The Ewoks freeze in horror at the sound of Darth Vader. Isn't he dead?

No, C-3PO tells them. He survived and in fact still lives!

"Mitka-gana!" groans the huntress, Asha Fahn.

STOMP! STOMP! STOMP! He stormed the rebels'

snow fortress with great metal monsters . . .

PZAP! PZAP! ZOOOOOM! But they escaped just in time on the *Millennium Falcon* . . .

SMASH SMASH CRASH! Only to find themselves stuck in an asteroid field! With TIE fighters close behind!

GULP! And then they were almost eaten by a giant space worm . . .

KERSHMASH! And then he, C-3PO, was blasted by stormtroopers on Cloud City!

WSHHHH-WSHHHH-WSHHHHH! And Darth Vader was there, too!

ZZZZZK! ZZZZK! And Luke fought him . . . but lost. *Nooooo!*

"Neesh Zon CHA!" moans Teebo.

WHOOSH! And they just barely got away on the *Falcon. . . .*

The Ewoks start to cheer, but C-3PO stops them.

Darth Vader and the Emperor have a new metal moon, he tells them, and points to the sky.

So that is what it is. The Ewoks have spent several

seasons wondering what is hanging in the sky over their forest.

And now they know.

It is a monster that kills not just forests, but whole worlds with fire.

"Neesh zon cha!" growls Chirpa. *"Neesh CHA GREE!"*

CHAPTER FORTY-EIGHT

✦

IN WHICH DARTH VADER ARRIVES ON THE FOREST MOON OF ENDOR

C-3PO SKIPS OVER many details—notably the many times he has wanted to give up during their adventures—but still his story takes a long time to tell.

Somewhere there in the middle, Luke Skywalker feels something—a mind reaching out to his mind through the flow of the Force—through the darkest parts of the Force.

It is his father. And Luke can feel that he is coming closer.

Vader is indeed getting closer every second, piloting his own shuttle down from the Death Star to the Imperial base that guards the shield generator.

Of all the Imperials who have completely ignored

the beauty of the forest moon of Endor, none have ever ignored it quite as fiercely as Vader does.

He swoops over the treetops and plunges into the heart of the dark forest seeing only the massive shield generator and its blazingly lit landing platform.

It's a hideous sight: a great industrial gash in the

midst of a beautiful forest; a tangle of pipes and wires and blast shields and bunkers.

But of course, Vader doesn't see the horror of it, only the purpose of it. The shields will protect the new Death Star until the Death Star is ready to bring order to the galaxy by destroying those parts that are not in order.

Vader hardly cares. His concerns are more personal. The Force is strong in his son, Luke. And Vader well knows that the Force is stronger than any Death Star.

Nothing matters until he has faced his son again.

And now, landing the shuttle and stomping down the ramp, he is close. Maddeningly close. Yet he can go no farther. The Emperor has told him to wait at the base.

Why wait? Why not summon his own stormtroopers, the 501st Legion? Why not lay waste to this whole forest and find his son *now*?

But there are other ways to search. So Vader searches with his mind. . . .

And he feels Luke's presence, and Luke feels his presence—a dark presence.

And Luke feels fear. He has known he must face Vader again. He has prepared himself for this. And yet the depth of the darkness that calls out to him is terrifying.

He fights to control his feelings. He leaves the

others, ducks out of the hut, and stands on a long bridge that stretches out into the gloom to one of the village's lesser trees.

From here Luke has a clear view of the new Death Star, one half smooth and armor plated, the other half a jagged mess of girders and half-built floors.

It is the most terrifying thing the galaxy has ever seen.

Yet there is something worse, closer, yet unseen, out there through the trees, on this moon . . . and looking for him.

And he knows he cannot hide from it.

CHAPTER FORTY-NINE

IN WHICH LEIA LEARNS
THE TRUTH AT LAST

AND THEN he is surprised by a light touch on his shoulder.

"Luke, what's wrong?"

It is Leia. He turns to look at her.

There is something else he can't hide from anymore: the truth.

"Leia . . . do you remember your mother? Your real mother?"

"Just a little bit. She died when I was very young."

"What do you remember?"

"Just . . . images, really," she says. "Feelings."

"Tell me."

"She was very beautiful. Kind . . . but sad," says Leia, but she is unsure how she knows this. Unsure, in fact, if she really did ever see her mother or just invented these memories to fill the hole in her life. "Why are you asking me this?"

"I have no memory of my mother. I never knew her."

"Luke, tell me. What's troubling you?"

Luke has been trying to. But it is so hard. The weight of learning that Vader is his father has almost crushed him. And now he is about to burden Leia with the same knowledge.

"Vader is here . . . now, on this moon."

Leia's first thought is the success of their mission. If Vader is here, it will be far more difficult. But why would Vader be here?

"How do you know?" she asks.

"I felt his presence. He's come for me. He can feel when I'm near. That's why I have to go."

"*Go?*"

"Yes . . . as long as I stay, I'm endangering the group and our mission here," he replies quietly. "I have to face him."

"Face him? Why?"

Luke has dreaded this moment, but now he finds relief as he finally lets loose his secret.

"He's my father."

"Your father?"

"There's more. It won't be easy for you to hear it, but you must. If I don't make it back, you're the only hope for the Alliance."

"Luke, don't talk that way. You have a power I . . . I don't understand and could never have."

Now he turns away from the forest at last. Turns to look at her. Through the light of smoking torches, he sees her clearly. He sees and senses her strength. Yes, he decides, she is strong enough to bear this. She, too, is a Skywalker after all.

"You're wrong, Leia. You have that power, too. In time, you'll learn to use it as I have. The Force is strong in my family. My father has it . . . I have it . . . and my sister has it."

And now a lot of things begin to make sense to Leia. Things that have never made sense before.

"Yes. It's you, Leia. You are my sister."

Yes, just like Luke, she feels the truth of this immediately. But what a truth to finally acknowledge! Finding out that Luke is her brother should bring her joy . . . but to learn that the dreaded Darth Vader—who captured her, imprisoned her, even tortured her—is her father? Alas, the joy of gaining a brother is lost for now in the shadow of their dark father.

"I know," she tells Luke. "Somehow . . . I've always known."

"Then you know why I have to face him."

"No!" she insists. "Luke, run away, far away. If he can feel your presence, then leave this place. I wish I could go with you."

"No, you don't. You've always been strong."

"But why must you confront him?"

This is the hardest question yet. He has long known he must, but is only beginning to understand why.

"Because . . . there is good in him. I've felt it.

He won't turn me over to the Emperor. I can save him. I can turn him back to the good side."

Even as he says this, his belief in it falters. Yoda told him he was wrong. Obi-Wan told him he was wrong.

"I have to try," he says.

And then he goes.

CHAPTER FIFTY

✦

IN WHICH OUR HEROES BECOME HONORARY EWOKS

BACK IN THE HUT, C-3PO has finished his story.

Chief Chirpa and his two best hunters, Teebo and Asha, are deep in discussion. Logray, the village shaman, tries to interrupt, which makes Asha growl and bare her teeth. But Chirpa stops her and lets Logray speak his mind. There's no need for us to get into a lot of Ewok politics now, but it's really a delicate business.

C-3PO's story has inspired Chief Chirpa to aid the rebels. But Logray has a different response: as a shaman, his first concern is the safety of the tribe. He thinks the Ewoks should stay out of matters that are obviously much bigger than themselves. Only with Teebo's and Asha's support is Chirpa able to overrule Logray. The shaman doesn't take it well and shakes his holy sticks and stones in frustration.

But when Chirpa makes his announcement and the whole village cheers, even Logray is caught up in the excitement. The Ewoks are ready to free their forest and help free the galaxy, too, even if they have only a vague idea what a galaxy is.

"*Neesh Chee Hidalg!*" Chirpa decrees.

"*Ooooo!*" the Ewoks respond, and then begin waving spears, banging drums, and attempting to embrace Chewbacca and Han.

"Wonderful!" exclaims C-3PO. "We are now a part of the tribe!"

"Just what I always wanted," says Han as Wicket clings to his leg.

"*Muurrug!*" groans Chewie as he tries to disentangle himself from all the little furry hugs.

"Well, short help is better than no help at all, Chewie."

With C-3PO translating, Han and the Ewoks agree to set out for the shield generator first thing in the morning. Hopefully the rest of the strike team will be waiting for them there and then it'll be all over but the shooting, thinks Han as he stretches out on the floor of Teebo's hut. Best to get some sleep first.

CHAPTER FIFTY-ONE

❂

IN WHICH LUKE CONFRONTS VADER

AT LAST!

Vader gets the call: a patrol has picked up a rebel spy in the woods.

It's his son. His destiny.

They're bringing the prisoner in on an AT-AT.*

Does Lord Vader want to wait here or . . .

Of course he doesn't want to wait! Out of his way, you fool!

He stomps off toward the AT-AT loading dock, two stormtroopers scurrying after him. He snarls his metallic snarl at various Imperial imbeciles who snap to attention as he storms past.

---

*You may recall these monstrous, four-legged metal walkers, and the smaller, two-legged AT-STs, from the Imperial attack on Hoth.

Then, as he thunders across a walkway, an elevator door opens at the other end and he sees Luke.

There he is! Defenseless. No visible weapon. Dressed in black cloth, no armor. Ah, yes, the boy has two hands again. But the hands are bound.

Vader could end all this right now. He could strike Luke down and be done—if not for his master's orders. He certainly feels enough hate to do it. Of course, we know, reader, that Vader's hate is not really hatred of Luke, but of his own past. But Vader has a fear of Luke, too. And fear and hate have long ruled this powerful Sith Lord.

"Lord Vader," says a smug Imperial officer who Vader hadn't noticed until this moment. There are two stormtroopers there as well presumably to guard the prisoner. How foolish they are.

"This is the rebel that surrendered to us," says the officer.

Vader sees the defiant look on Luke's face. He knows this is no surrender. This will be a great struggle.

Vader says nothing so the officer continues:

"Although he denies it, I believe there may be more of them, and I request permission to conduct a further search of the area."

Again Vader says nothing, so the officer is forced to give up his last piece of information.

"He was armed only with this," he tells Vader, holding out Luke's lightsaber.

"Good work, Commander," says Vader, taking the weapon. "Leave us. Conduct your search and bring his companions to me."

"Yes, my lord," says the officer, less smug than he was. He and the troopers step back into the elevator and now at last Vader and Luke meet again.

But Vader turns from Luke. His mission is not to engage in a battle—either of weapons or words—but only to bring Luke back to his master.

"The Emperor has been expecting you."

"I know, Father," says Luke, eager to turn this meeting to his own purpose.

"So, you have accepted the truth."

"I've accepted the truth that you were once Anakin Skywalker, my father."

Now Vader does face him.

"That name no longer has any meaning for me," he booms, looming over Luke.

But Luke answers with compassion, not fear.

"It is the name of your true self. You've only forgotten. I know there is good in you. The Emperor hasn't driven it from you fully. That was why you couldn't destroy me. That's why you won't bring me to your Emperor now."

The struggle is already greater than Vader expected. He turns away again, this time looking at the lightsaber in his hand. This is not his old lightsaber, he realizes. Where has this come from?

He ignites it. Admires the focused green light. A flick of his wrist would kill Luke now, but that doesn't even occur to him.

"I see you have constructed a new lightsaber. Your skills are complete. Indeed, you are powerful, as the Emperor has foreseen."

But Luke isn't going to be distracted.

"Come with me," he says.

Now Vader truly understands why he has feared his son so much. Not because of his mastery of the Force or skill with a lightsaber. But because Luke can make him question the dark truths that have long ruled him.

Defensively, he recites these truths now . . . even as he begins to wonder if they really are true.

"Obi-Wan once thought as you do. You don't know the power of the dark side. I must obey my master."

"I will not turn . . . and you'll be forced to kill me."

"If that is your destiny . . ."

It is a cold answer. Especially from a father to a son. But it is also a weak one. And Luke knows it. He presses his attack.

"Search your feelings, Father. You can't do this. I feel the conflict within you. Let go of your hate."

Luke's attack has at last reached into the great,

dark, troubled mind of Anakin Skywalker. And to Vader it is far more painful than the lightsaber slash Luke scored in Cloud City.

But even this is not enough, Luke. Ah, they all tried to warn you: the dark side is strong. Vader uses it to close off the questions, the memories, the hopes. The dark truths are true again.

"It is too late for me, son. The Emperor will show you the true nature of the Force. *He* is your master now."

Vader turns abruptly and signals two of his two stormtroopers to come take the prisoner.

The battle is over and Luke has lost.

"Then my father is truly dead," he says as he is prodded toward the landing pad.

Yes, Luke did lose this battle, but once he has gone, we can see that Vader has lost something, too. He stares out at the trees, no longer so impatient for action.

CHAPTER FIFTY-TWO

✦

IN WHICH THE NIGHT PASSES SLOWLY ON ENDOR

SOON THE SHUTTLE carries Luke to the Death Star, leaving behind his friends—who are, of course, not going to be found by that smug Imperial officer who has no idea at all that they are hiding in a treetop Ewok village.

This forest moon turns rather slowly and the night is a long one. Especially for Leia, who has far too much to think about to sleep.

Han is restless, too. He feels the heavy responsibility of leading the strike team tomorrow. If the strike team is even out there, that is. For all he knows they've been captured or killed or . . . Things were so much more fun when it was just him and Chewie and no worries.

Chewbacca isn't particularly worried, but he certainly isn't comfortable, either. Forget about squeezing into an Ewok bed, he can barely even fit in an Ewok hut. He grumbles and mumbles all night.

The Ewoks aren't asleep, either.

They are holding a council of war.

Things are said that are not cute. The Ewoks are talking of battle, of weapons and traps and death.

These are fierce creatures. Predators. The top of the food chain in a deadly forest. And they are ready to kill.

For, you see, now that the Ewoks understand that our heroes are in fact heroes—and are there to destroy the cursed biker scouts and blow up the great metal mess in the sky—they are eager to help. They had known nothing of the great galactic struggle for freedom that the Rebellion had carried on for decades.

But, Chirpa reminds them, they did know that a great evil had come to their forest. He recalls the tribe members killed by the Empire's soldiers and metal monsters.

Several of the Ewoks here are refugees whose villages were destroyed when the Empire arrived to build its sprawling generator and troop base. Chirpa calls on one of these, Romba, to tell of the night he returned from hunting to find his village burning and his whole tribe dead.

The Ewoks have heard this story before with fear. But Chirpa tells them it must now give them something to fight for, not hide from.

Now, he tells them, the tribe has a new hope. These strangers believe that the Empire can be beaten and he believes it, too. But . . . he warns that the strangers cannot win without the Ewoks' help.

"Then let us help them," declares Asha. They have fought to protect their territory before, and now the whole forest is at stake.

"This is bigger than one tribe of Ewoks," agrees Romba. "Tomorrow's battle will affect all Ewoks. So all Ewoks should have the chance to join in."

Logray mumbles something about some sacred refuge where they could hide, but no one else is interested.

So in the end, Chirpa's decision is really the village's decision.

He sends messengers off through the forest to explain it all to the leaders of other tribes . . . and ask for their help. The message, composed by Teebo, is beautifully worded in the Ewok language, but C-3PO translates it somewhat mechanically, like this: "Tomorrow we fight to save our forest and bring down the cold metal moon. Our new golden god has shown us how. Join us and we will be free again."*

What Han Solo, who is the commander of this mission after all, would have said about all this we'll

---

*Again, the original Ewok version is much more moving, and all those who heard it, even Logray, were given hope and resolve.

never know, because he and Chewie had finally fallen asleep.

Leia sleeps at last, the chaos in her mind quieted by exhaustion.

Even R2 and C-3PO have powered down, to save energy for the coming action.

And perhaps we, too, should pause, reader . . . because when the sun rises tomorrow, things are going to get crazy. There will be no more plodding. The plodding is over.

So . . . take a deep breath and when you're ready we'll make the jump to lightspeed.

THE
POWER
OF THE
DARK SIDE!

CHAPTER FIFTY-THREE

IN WHICH ACKBAR LAUNCHES THE REBEL FLEET

FAR AWAY, the rebel fleet is a swarming hive no more. It is lined up, every ship pointing across the galaxy toward the distant Death Star.

"Admiral, we're in position," Lando says, leaning over the *Millennium Falcon*'s controls to speak into the comlink. "All fighters accounted for."

"Proceed with the countdown. All groups assume attack coordinates," comes the crackling response from Admiral Ackbar on the bridge of the command ship, the Mon Calamari vessel known as *Home One*.

Nien Nunb, in the *Falcon*'s copilot seat, chatters as he taps the coordinates into the computer.

"Don't worry, they'll have that shield down," says

Lando, then murmurs, "or this will be the shortest attack of all time."

Nien Nunb responds with his own muttered comment, but finishes his task, flips a switch, and settles back into his seat.

"All craft, prepare to jump into hyperspace on my mark," Ackbar orders, his voice going out to the entire fleet now.

"For the Rebellion . . . and for the Republic . . . *now!*"

Nien Nunb pulls a lever and he and Lando watch the galaxy both stretch and shrink as the hyperdrive engines propel the *Falcon* and the rest of the fleet at such a speed that the stars streak past.

But wait: it wasn't the whole fleet. One ship is left behind: Mon Mothma's ship. In a moment, she will order it to take her to a safe hiding place to await news. But for now she stares out at the vast emptiness and hopes.

CHAPTER FIFTY-FOUR

✦

IN WHICH TWO DROIDS TRIP AND STUMBLE THROUGH A FOREST

WHEN OUR HEROES AWAKE, they find the village nearly deserted. There were an abundance of very young and very old Ewoks, but all those able to join the fight had risen and followed Chirpa, Teebo, and Asha into the forest. There was much work to be done.

Wicket tries to explain this to C-3PO, who tries to explain it to Solo, who doesn't quite grasp the importance of the words. The important thing to him is that a few Ewoks—Romba, Wicket, and Paploo*—are

---

*Romba is the "official" guide. Chirpa decreed that Wicket and Paploo were too young to join the main Ewok fighting force, but if he thinks they're going to just sit around the village all day, he's crazy.

still there to help them find the easiest way to the rendezvous point.

Even with the Ewoks' help, it is a frustrating journey with C-3PO seeming to fall over every root or clump of ferns and R2 needing to be lifted over dead logs. Leia has to remind Solo—who has, I fear, uttered some impolite language—how useful the droids have been already.

And in any case, it is quite necessary to have R2, since he is best able to home in on the coordinates of the rendezvous site, which they eventually do . . . albeit with very little time to spare.

The rebel strike team is indeed there. Solo feels a little foolish introducing them to the Ewoks, but these soldiers are all veterans and they know the importance of having someone on a mission who understands the lay of the land.

And that's exactly what Romba can offer them. He, unlike any of the other Ewoks, is a native of this part of the forest. His village once stood not far from here and he knows every tree and every path.

First he leads the team to a bit of high ground. From here Solo gets his first look at the military base and shield generator that he has promised to destroy.

It is an intimidating site: a complex of industrial buildings sprawling under an enormous landing pad and even more enormous shield-casters. An AT-AT stomps around near the only entrance gate, while several AT-STs bustle about importantly. Guard towers top the thick, high wall and biker scouts zip about in front of it.

Chewie lets out a low growl and Solo and Leia exchange looks. There's muttering among the troops, and that's never a good sign.

"The control bunker's on the far side of that landing platform," says Leia. "This isn't going to be easy."

"Hey, don't worry," responds Solo, "Chewie and me have got into a lot of places more heavily guarded than this."

But Leia knows Solo's bluster, by now. And she knows that he's as worried as she is.

Romba tugs at Leia's sleeve, chattering away.

"What's he saying?" she asks C-3PO.

And now, reader, we see how even a protocol droid can play a pivotal role in a galactic war. What a chain of chance that brought C-3PO here—built by young Anakin on Tatooine, hauled back and forth across the galaxy on missions he never quite understood, blasted to bits on Cloud City, picked at by Salacious Crumb, stumbling, tripping, plodding, and always complaining and almost always left behind—he has somehow made it here to the middle of this forest where he can save the lives of the whole strike team with the power of his six-million-language interpreting system.

Chance? Or the Force? Or just the old Han Solo luck? We really don't have time to get into it now, because C-3PO is listening to Romba and announcing: "He says there's a secret entrance on the other side of the ridge."

Well, that changes everything!

"A back door, eh? Good idea," says Solo, greatly relieved.

Half an hour later, the strike team has reassembled in another part of the forest and Solo and Leia survey the scene from behind a fallen log.

A low bunker is built into a hill. True, it has a thick, Imperial-standard blast door . . . but our heroes have the code, thanks to the Bothan spies.

And here the only guards are four biker scouts. Four rather bored biker scouts, in fact. They've been stationed back here for months without seeing the least bit of action and they're currently leaning against the bunker complaining about it, as bored troopers are wont to do.

"Thank goodness," says Leia, "we're running out of time."

"It's only a few guards. This shouldn't be too much trouble," says Han.

"Well, it only takes one to sound the alarm."

"Then we'll do it real quiet-like," says Solo with

a grin that is so perfectly self-confident that it really deserves a clever description, but again there is no time, because the grin disappears a second later when C-3PO interrupts.

"Oh! Oh, my!"

"Quiet," hiss Leia and Solo at the same time, but C-3PO isn't just complaining this time.

"I'm afraid our furry companion has gone and done something rather rash." He points and they turn back to the bunker just in time to see Paploo scramble onto a speeder bike, flip some switches, possibly at random, and go roaring away into the forest, clinging to the handlebars, lasers blasting and repulsorlift engines screeching.

"EE CHEE WA MAA!"

"There goes our surprise attack," groans Solo.

"Whhuug," agrees Chewie.

But they're both wrong.

Three of the four scouts jump onto the three remaining bikes and shoot off after Paploo, who leads them on a merry—if somewhat death-defying—chase through the trees before grabbing hold of a vine to swing unnoticed and unharmed up into a tree, while his speeder bike—and the troopers on their bikes—streak on through the forest.

"Not bad for a little furball," says Han, as the speeder bikes disappear into the trees. "Only one guard left. Let's go."

He turns to go, then remembers that he still wants to do this quietly. He turns back and points at R2-D2 and C-3PO. "Stay here!"

Han and Chewie sneak up behind the distracted, bikeless guard, while Leia leads the strike team toward the bunker.

R2 gives a low whistle and rocks impatiently, but C-3PO doesn't budge. "I have decided that we shall stay here."

CHAPTER FIFTY-FIVE

✦

IN WHICH LUKE FACES
THE EMPEROR

L**UKE FAILED** to turn his father away from the dark side on Endor. And now, in the far less pleasant setting of the Death Star's throne room, he must face the consequences of that failure. Vader has brought him here so that the Emperor can turn Luke to the dark side.

You may think that there's not a chance of such a thing, but that is only because you, like Luke, have underestimated the Emperor and the dark force that has consumed him.

"Welcome, young Skywalker. I have been expecting you." The voice comes from deep within a dark hood. There's just enough light for Luke to see the Emperor's twisted, hateful smile.

"You no longer need those binders," says the Emperor, and with the twitching of one of his gnarled fingers they fall to the ground. Luke is free to attack now.

"Guards, leave us," calls the Emperor, and his silent, red protectors glide away.* Now, Luke is even more free to attack.

"His lightsaber," booms Vader, handing the deadly weapon to his master.

"Ah, yes, a Jedi's weapon. Much like your father's," says the Emperor, carelessly laying the lightsaber on the armrest of his throne.

Now the way is fully clear for Luke to attack. And surely he must be thinking of it. But he does not.

The Emperor goes on. . . .

"By now you must know your father can never be

---

*The Emperor doesn't really feel the need to be guarded. He only keeps these guards around to impress visitors. Now that they've been seen, they are free to take the service elevator down to their break room and take off their ridiculous helmets until called upon again.

turned from the dark side. So will it be with you."

"It is pointless to resist, my son," says Vader, looming behind Luke.

"I'm looking forward to completing your training," says the Emperor. "In time you will call me Master."

"You're gravely mistaken," replies Luke calmly. "You won't convert me as you did my father."

The Emperor looks up and Luke sees his eyes for the first time. Anger and hate burn in them and Palpatine's smile grows even worse.

"Oh, no, my young Jedi. You will find that it is you who are mistaken . . . about a great many things."

"You're wrong. Soon I'll be dead . . . and you with me."

And now comes something worse than the Emperor's smile, his laugh. A nasty little laugh, meant to irritate and offend.

"Perhaps you refer to the imminent attack of your rebel fleet," the Emperor says casually.

Luke freezes. This was unexpected. Just as the Emperor wanted it to be.

"Yes . . . I assure you we are quite safe from your friends here," croaks the Emperor, savoring the moment.

"Your overconfidence is your weakness," declares Luke, struggling to control his fear that the rebel fleet is indeed doomed.

"Your faith in your friends is yours!" snarls the Emperor. "Everything that has transpired has done so according to my design."

The Emperor turns slightly and gestures out the magnificent window behind his throne. Luke looks out and sees a cloudy green ball hanging in the empty starfield.

"Your friends up there on the forest moon are walking into a trap. As is your rebel fleet! It was I who allowed the Alliance to know the location of the shield generator. It is quite safe from your pitiful little band. An entire legion of my best troops awaits them."

Now the fear in Luke's heart grows—they are doomed! And the fear quickly turns to anger. He whirls back to face the Emperor but his gaze lands on his weapon. Oh, how quickly the Emperor has brought out Luke's own dark side! And now to push him just a little further. . . .

"Oh . . . I'm afraid the deflector shield will be quite operational when your friends arrive."

CHAPTER FIFTY-SIX

✦

IN WHICH ALL GOES AS THE EMPEROR HAS PLANNED

NOW YOU MAY BE THINKING that the Emperor is lying. He's very good at that after all. As Senator, and then Chancellor, and now Emperor Palpatine, he has built his entire Empire on lies.*

But not this time. This time the Emperor has told the truth. And Han and Leia are about to learn that firsthand.

Han got them into the bunker easily enough. First he tricked the only remaining guard into chasing him around the corner of the bunker . . .

---

*Yes, there were deadly robots and killer clones and Order 66 and Inquisitors and all that. But those are just the details. The real heart of the Empire is deceit and betrayal.

where the whole strike team was waiting with weapons drawn.

And then he tapped the Bothan's stolen code into the bunker's door and that slid open, revealing a control room full of engineers and computer operators, without a soldier in sight.

"All right, up! C'mon! Move! Quickly!" yells Han, waving his blaster. His strike team rushes in behind him to take charge of the prisoners.

"The charges, Chewie! Quickly!" he calls, and the two of them begin attaching thermal detonators in strategic locations around the room.

But what was it the Emperor said? Didn't he mention a legion of his best troops? Where are they?

Blast doors whizz open and the stormtroopers surge in from the corridors where they've been waiting. More pour in from outside.

"Freeze, you rebel scum!" snarls their commander.

And Han has no choice. Dozens of blaster rifles

are pointed at him. No action, no matter how brave, could save the day here. There isn't even a chance to trigger the bombs.

He looks at Chewie and Leia. They are as helpless as he is.

It's all over.

CHAPTER FIFTY-SEVEN

✦

IN WHICH THE REBELS' BEAUTIFUL PLAN TURNS INTO CHAOS

HIGH ABOVE THE MOON, the rebel fleet emerges from hyperspace with a silent pop.

Leading the charge, Lando and Nien Nunb look through the *Falcon*'s cockpit window at the giant Death Star dead ahead. It's bigger than either imagined. And only gets bigger as they zoom toward it.

Lando leans toward the comlink, making sure the rest of the fleet is behind him.

"All wings, report in."

The answers crackle back to him:

"Red Leader standing by."

"Gray Leader standing by."

"Green Leader standing by."

"Lock S-foils in attack positions," Wedge tells his squadron of X-wings.

"May the Force be with us," comes the voice of Admiral Ackbar.

"Ah-the-yairee u-hareh mu-ah-hareh," cries Nien Nunb, urgently pointing at a control panel.

"What?" yells Lando. "We've got to be able to get some kind of a reading on that shield, up or down!"

"Mu-ah-hareh mu-kay, huh? E-mutee bit-chu me!" fusses the copilot.

"Well, how can they be jamming our transmission if they don't know we're coming?"

They look at each other, then at the Death Star.

"Break off the attack," Lando yells into the comlink as he yanks the controls to one side. "The shield is still up!"

"I get no reading," Wedge calls over the comlink. "Are you sure?"

"Pull up!" yells Lando. "All craft, pull up!"

The maneuverable *Falcon* and X-wings peel away

just before hitting the shield. The larger craft have a tougher time making the turn.

"Take evasive action!" bellows Ackbar over the comlink. And then he calls to his own crew, "Port engines, full reverse!" sending the ship into a shuddering, lurching spin, but saving it from smashing to bits on the invisible barrier, which, as the Emperor promised, is still quite operational.

"Green group! Stick close to holding sector MV-Seven," he commands, but it's not going to be that easy to regroup!

"Admiral!" yells a controller, pointing to a view-screen. "We have enemy ships in sector forty-seven."

Ackbar looks up expecting to see a few TIE fighters. Instead, he sees a whole fleet: ten, eleven, maybe more Star Destroyers—and one Super Star Destroyer—shooting out from their hiding place behind the moon, each one unleashing a swarm of TIE fighters.

"It's a trap!"

CHAPTER FIFTY-EIGHT

✦

IN WHICH THE EMPEROR
FEELS A DARK JOY

"**COME, BOY,** see for yourself," croaks the Emperor, and Luke can't help obeying. He walks closer to the window and sees the trap being sprung.

The Imperial fleet splits open like the rancor's jaws to crush and swallow the rebels.

At this distance, the deaths of individual X-wing pilots are nothing more than brief red flashes. It's all silent. It's all out there in the vacuum of space on the other side of this meter-thick glass.

"From here you will witness the final destruction of the Alliance," spits the Emperor, "and the end of your insignificant Rebellion."

And Luke can do nothing! Or can he? His eyes

flick back to the throne. His lightsaber is still there.

Ah, but the Emperor has been waiting for this. He finds space battles rather dull, but the battle here in the throne room is what really brings him joy.

He pats the lightsaber almost lovingly with his gnarled hand. And he smiles.

"You want this, don't you? The hate is swelling in you now. Take your weapon. Use it. I am unarmed. Strike me down with it."

Luke turns back to the window, but the Emperor knows he is still thinking about the lightsaber.

"Give in to your anger. With each passing moment, you make yourself more my servant."

"No," says Luke, turning to face the two Sith Lords.

"It is unavoidable. It is your destiny," the Emperor says gently. "You, like your father, are now mine."

Luke looks at his father—standing obediently by the throne, silent except for the continual clicks and wheezes of his respirator—and then he turns back to the window. What he sees there is a nightmare.

CHAPTER FIFTY-NINE

✪

IN WHICH THE *FALCON* FLIES INTO THE NIGHTMARE

"**T**HERE'S TOO MANY OF THEM!" screams someone through the comlink.

Lando doesn't know who and there's no time to find out and it hardly matters. There *are* too many of them.

There has never been a battle like this before. Any time that the Empire has had this many ships in one place, the rebels have always been careful to be as far away as possible.

But now they've been lured here to face far more ships than expected. For each rebel fighter there is a pack of TIE fighters out to hunt it down. For each mid-sized rebel cruiser there is a monstrous Star

Destroyer bristling with cannons and torpedoes.

But don't give up hope, reader. Not every ship is created equal and the rebels have the ship that did the Kessel Run in less than twelve parsecs. The fastest hunk of junk in the galaxy: the *Millennium Falcon*.

And at the controls are two of the best pilots in the galaxy, Lando and Nien Nunb.

And that's a good thing, because even a small space battle is not an easy thing to fly through. Ships, laser bolts, proton torpedoes racing toward you from every direction. Meanwhile, you're racing toward other ships, laser bolts, and proton torpedoes at egregious speeds. And every time you change course you risk flying into a different set of ships, laser bolts, and proton torpedoes that were minding their own business but are now more than happy to blow up your ship.

And speaking of ships blowing up, that happens a lot, and you have to make sure you don't run into the explosions . . . or the drifting debris that floats about afterward.

Now add in the fact that you aren't just dodging all this stuff, but actively trying to protect your friends and blast away at your enemies. And now multiply all that times a thousand as Lando finesses his way through the whole Imperial armada.

When dealing with all this, it helps if you're using the Force, like Luke, but Lando doesn't have that power. What does he have? Nothing but the courage to fly faster and cut things closer than the enemy dares.

And right now he's cutting it awfully close. He's chasing down a TIE fighter even while three others are roaring in from behind. He really should break off his attack and try to get the *Falcon* out of this mess.

Instead, he increases speed and takes a new angle, racing to cut the TIE fighter off by short-cutting insanely close to the bow of a rebel cruiser.

Just before impact, Lando does a hard roll, barely
squeaking past the other ship.*

The risky maneuver brought them in close

---

*If we could pause the battle, get out a ruler, and measure just
how close the *Falcon* came to destruction, even Lando would be
disturbed by the answer. I fear he has already broken his "not a
scratch" promise.

enough to not only blow up the TIE they were chasing, but also double back and, thanks to some fancy shooting by Nien Nunb, pick off the two others, while Lando just barely avoided the stray fire from three TIEs chasing an X-wing across their path.

"Watch yourself, Wedge!" cries Lando. "Three from above!"

"Red Three! Red Two! Pull in!"

"Got it!"

"Two more coming in, twenty degrees!"

"Cut to the left! I'll take the leader!" calls Wedge.

Lando forces the *Falcon* into a flip and Nien Nunb unleashes a broadside on the pack of TIEs. Two explode, but the other three cut away in time and now streak toward one of the larger ships.

"They're heading for the medical frigate!" cries Wedge.

They give chase, weaving in and out of the absolute chaos of a thousand ships pulling—or trying to pull—the same sort of aerial tricks.

Wedge does knock out the leader, but not before two X-wings are shot down and the *Falcon* takes a brutal hit to its forward deflectors.

And still more TIE fighters swoop in, bombarding the frigate until the hull starts to crack.

"Lamou-be-o-tee," growls Nien Nunb.

"I know it," yells Lando, "but what else can we—"

But he stops because he's just answered his own question. Somehow in all that mess of flying and shooting and being shot at, he managed to pull off a quick bit of thinking.

"We've got to draw their fire off our cruisers," he orders into the comlink. "Accelerate to attack speed and follow me!"

"Copy, Gold Leader," answers Wedge, and what's left of the rebel fighter squadrons turns to fly directly at the largest Star Destroyer in the Imperial fleet.

Seconds later, a horde of TIE fighters is rushing to meet their attack.

The two forces of fighters collide in a furious cloud of ships, laser bolts, and proton torpedoes, flying in and out and around and sometimes into the Star Destroyers.

Lando's plan has worked. He has brought the battle to the Empire now and he keeps bringing it in closer. Hardened Imperial officers find themselves shrinking back from their windows as the rebel pilots skim the surface of the Star Destroyer, blasting everything in sight.

There are minor victories for the rebels in this new round of chaos . . . but they are very, very minor. And the Imperial fleet is very, very large.

It's still just a matter of time until the strength of the rebel fleet is exhausted and the endless might of the Empire wins the day as it has won every day for a generation.

Unless . . .

CHAPTER SIXTY

✦

IN WHICH AN IMPROBABLE IDEA IS DISCUSSED

UNLESS . . . WELL . . . you don't suppose? You know . . . the Ewoks?

I mean, everybody else is basically captured, trapped, or doomed at this point.

Maybe they could . . .

No, no, it's impossible.

Well . . . maybe not impossible, but highly improbable. But then again, Han Solo always says, "Never tell me the odds."

That's not what he's saying right this second, of course. Right this second, he's being shoved out of the bunker by a squad of stormtroopers only to find the rest of the legion waiting for him in the clearing.

But when he does get a chance to say it, what he means is, don't rule something out just because it seems unlikely.

And the idea of the Ewoks having any effect at all on this giant galactic war is the most unlikely idea of all.

Han and Leia haven't even thought of it. And the biker scouts and stormtroopers would get a good laugh out of it. And we already know how the Emperor just waved aside the whole species.

And of course, C-3PO thinks the idea is madness, but he thinks that about everything.

R2, however, has thought it over—in his own astromech way of thinking things over—and he rather likes it—in his own astromech way of liking things.

"*Beepbaleep WHIRR!*"

"Oh, Artoo, really? Do you really think I should? Commander Solo told us to wait quietly. He said nothing about us being involved in a rescue."

"*Brreep beepaleep WHIRRRR!*"

"Well! I just think we should—"

R2 interrupts with a wild, ear-splitting series of beeps and whoops. A hundred stormtroopers turn to look. They see C-3PO stumble out from behind a tree, closely followed by R2.

"Up there on the ridge!" a commander barks. "Bring those two down here."

The closest cluster of troopers trots over to the tree to capture the droids.

"Well, they're on their way, Artoo. Are you sure this was a good idea?"

"Bzrreee-whee!"

"Freeze, don't move," orders the first of the troopers to arrive.

"Oh, we surrender! We surrender!" assures C-3PO with his hands up.

So far this has all been rather likely. Are you ready for the unlikely part? The idea so unlikely that even the Emperor couldn't foresee it?

Well, I hope you are ready because . . .

"MIRRRRCHIWAWAAAAA!"

As the troopers step forward to deactivate the droids, a net, closely followed by a band of Ewoks, drops from the tree limbs above.

Tangled in the net and encumbered with too much armor, the stormtroopers are rather easy prey for the Ewoks.

Not to go into too much detail, but while stormtrooper armor is indeed stronger than either Ewoks or Ewok weapons . . . there are joints in the armor, small gaps just about the right size for, say, Teebo's spear.

And as for that small gap at the neck, between the helmet and the shoulder armor . . . well that's just about the size of the razor-sharp knife that Romba made from the tooth of a boar-wolf he slew.

"Oooooh! Stand back, Artoo," C-3PO calls as the slaughter begins.*

---

*Perhaps we should stand back, too. It's going to be messy.

CHAPTER SIXTY-ONE

✦

IN WHICH THE EWOKS SOUND
THEIR HUNTING HORNS

REMEMBER ALL those troopers and biker scouts and big equipment that were guarding the main gate earlier?

That's what we're up against now.

And the Ewoks are looking down on all this from the treetops. Looking down at more soldiers and war machines than they've ever seen or ever imagined.

It would be easy, sensible even, for the Ewoks to sit quietly up in the branches and not get into a fight with this great horde of evil.

But don't make the same mistake the Emperor did. Don't underestimate them!

High in a tree, an Ewok blows a long, ominous note on a hollow horn.

Burrwhoooooooo!

From near and far come answering calls.

Burrrwhooo! Burwhooo! Burwhooooo!

From the trees all around the edges of the clearing, Ewoks shoot arrows and drop rocks onto the crowd of troopers below. The arrows are relatively ineffective, except when they strike an unarmored officer. But the rocks, dropped from such a height, are enough to knock a stormtrooper out of commission for a while. There will be time to finish them off later, figure the Ewoks . . . and who knows? They may be tasty.

Even when the troopers realize where the rocks are coming from, they can only fire aimlessly into the leaves.

When more Ewoks pop up behind a ridge to fire arrows, the troopers find easier targets. Several Ewoks fall, but most retreat back into the undergrowth.

The troopers charge, the biker scouts hit their accelerators, and the four AT-STs stomp after them, too. But what they don't realize is that once they leave their little manmade clearing by the bunker, they are entering the Ewoks' forest. And right now that forest is one big trap.

BRRRRWHOOOOOO!

Troopers find themselves caught in nets or tumbling into pits before they can get a clean shot at the furry creatures scampering through the brush.

Biker scouts run into vines stretched between trees or lose control after getting clonked on the head by a bolo. One meets a nasty fate when a vine is looped over his front stabilizers, wrenching him into the nearest tree.

Even the AT-STs run into trouble. One AT-ST commander spots some Ewoks trying to set up some kind of catapult. While his gunner blasts away at the device, the commander twists the controls to send the great metal walker rushing to the spot.

The catapult is destroyed, but seconds later so is the AT-ST, as two logs swing down from the trees and crush the cockpit betwixt them.

And where there are no traps set, the Ewoks get by on instinct—biting, clawing, swarming, climbing, hiding, and then lunging out to do it all again. Alas, many are dying, but few fall who have not first struck some blow against the monsters in their forest.

And every Imperial that so much as stumbles, finds himself covered in angry Ewoks, each one looking for that spot to slip a knife through the armor.

"Mirchiwaawa!" screams Teebo, plunging his blade into—well, let's not say exactly where. But as he raises his blood-drenched fist into the air in triumph, the rest of his tribe answers: *"Mirchiwawaaaa!"*

And the other tribes take up the call, too! And the forest rings with their fury!

CHAPTER SIXTY-TWO

✦

IN WHICH OUR HEROES
ARE BACK IN ACTION

IMPERIAL OFFICERS, ducking a constant barrage of arrows, have been sending more and more troopers into the forest to put a stop to it all.

Now only a dozen or so troopers remain to guard the prisoners. But surely that's enough to handle—

BRRRRWHOOOO!

Another horn blows and Asha leads the tribe's fiercest warriors in a mad leap from atop the bunker.

"Mircheeewawaaaaaaa!" she screams as she lands on the back of an Imperial officer, reaching her wicked hunting knife over his shoulder and—well, never mind what she did next. The important thing is that the officer doesn't even have time to

shout a command to his confused troopers.

As the stormtroopers try to fend off their tiny attackers, Han and Chewie hurl themselves at the closest guards and the chaos is complete. Leia and the rest of the strike team charge in to grab the guns away from their distracted captors.

"*GRRRRHHHWGRRR!*" Chewie lets loose a Wookiee war cry as he clobbers the trooper who had confiscated his bowcaster. Raising the mighty weapon, he begins blasting away and charges into the woods after the fleeing troopers.

The strike team takes up positions on each side of the bunker, and for the moment, the bunker entrance belongs to the rebels. Unfortunately, the bunker door does not. It has closed again.

Han punches in the code, but nothing happens.

"The code's changed!"* he hollers to Leia.

---

*Imperial officers usually don't get much credit for quick thinking. But you really have to hand it to the one who thought of changing the door code after the trap was sprung. That was clever. Evil, but clever.

"We need Artoo!" she yells back.

"Artoo! Where are you! We need you right away!" Han barks into his comlink.

Not far from where we left them, R2 and C-3PO are relatively safe behind a log.

"Beek-ull-deep," chirps R2 matter-of-factly, and rolls out into the clearing.

"Going? What do you mean, going?" calls C-3PO. "This is no time for heroics! Come back!"

But of course, R2 doesn't come back and C-3PO, yet again, has no choice but to follow. Or does he have a choice? After all, couldn't he stay hidden behind the log, too? Is it possible that after all he's been through his circuits have developed something along the lines of bravery?

Whatever the answer, he and R2 head across the clearing, which, I'm sorry to say, is now buzzing with blaster fire as some regrouped stormtroopers launch an assault on the rearmed strike team.

"Oh dear!"

CHAPTER SIXTY-THREE

✵

IN WHICH THE EMPEROR HAS YET ANOTHER TRICK TO PLAY

HIGH ABOVE THE ENDOR moon another battle still rages.

Lando and the rebel fighter pilots have succeeded in drawing the fire away from the rebel fleet, but the cost has been great. Their fleet gets smaller and smaller every minute and yet they hardly seem to be making a dent in the enemy's fleet.

Still, it could have been worse. Lando had worried that the Star Destroyers would use their countless cannons to pick off the X-wings, but so far that hasn't happened.

"Only their fighters are attacking," he mutters,

half to Nien Nunb and half to himself. "I wonder what those Star Destroyers are waiting for."

The commander of the *Eclipse*, the Emperor's own Super Star Destroyer, is wondering the same thing. He has maneuvered the ship slightly away from the battle and now has a clear shot at the rebel cruisers, including Ackbar's command ship.

"We're in attack position now, sir," he tells Admiral Piett.

"Hold here," says Piett.

"We're not going to attack?"

"I have my orders from the Emperor himself. He has something special planned for them. We only need to keep them from escaping."

Was there a bit of a sigh as Piett gave that explanation? There was certainly a look of disappointment on the commander's face.

Neither of these officers would ever complain about an order that came directly from the Emperor.

But the whole thing seems rather anticlimactic.

Both men have been chasing these rebels their whole careers. Piett, in particular, has his reasons for wanting to beat Ackbar once and for all. And now here he is with the Mon Calamari ship in his sights and he isn't allowed to pull the trigger.

"What *is* the Emperor up to?" he wonders.

The Emperor is up to no good, as you can imagine, reader.

He's had a delightful time watching both Luke and the rebel fleet crumbling at the same time. But now . . . it's time to smash them both.

"As you can see, my young apprentice, your friends have failed."

Luke doesn't even turn around. He's not ready to admit that his friends have failed and he's certainly not ready to be called "my young apprentice."

But the Emperor knows his words have caused pain. And he knows what he says next will cause so much more.

"Now witness the firepower of this fully armed and operational battle station."

Now Luke does turn to look at him in surprise. The Emperor leans forward as he presses a button on his armrest.

"You may fire when ready, Commander."

Far away, in the Death Star's control room, Jerjerrod hears the command.

You remember Jerjerrod, of course. He's the one who told himself the new Death Star's massive cannon would never need to be used. Ah, if we only had time to reflect on how this not particularly bad man ended up doing this evil deed.

But we don't. Because this evil deed only takes one word.

"Fire!"

Out in space, there is a mighty flash and one of the larger rebel ships, *The Liberty*, is suddenly and silently gone. In its place swirls a cloud of dust and debris and death.

"That blast came from the Death Star!" Lando yells into the comlink. "That thing's operational!"

"We saw it. All craft, prepare to retreat!" commands Ackbar.

Retreat? Lando has never liked that word. And this time it means abandoning his friends on the Endor moon and leaving the Death Star intact and the Empire as strong as ever, all to limp away with half the ships they came with. And then what would they do? Hide?

"You won't get another chance at this, Admiral."

"We have no choice, General Calrissian. Our cruisers can't repel firepower of that magnitude."

"Then you'll need to move in closer to the Star Destroyers."

"Closer, General?"

"Yes! I said *closer*. Move as close as you can and engage those Star Destroyers at point-blank range."

Ackbar is not used to being yelled at over a comlink or being told what to do. But Lando does have a point. The Death Star wouldn't dare shoot into its own fleet. Still, it seems crazy to tangle directly with a Star Destroyer.

"At that close range," he tells Lando, sensibly, "we won't last long against those Star Destroyers."

"We'll last longer than we will against that Death Star! Han will have that shield down, we've just got to give him more time."

CHAPTER SIXTY-FOUR

✦

IN WHICH TIME TICKS AWAY

JUST TO BE CLEAR, R2 is *not* plodding. He is rolling as fast as he can considering the terrain. But it certainly *seems* like he is plodding to Han and Leia.

"Come on! Come on!" yells Han.

"Oh, Artoo, hurry," calls C-3PO, scuttling past the smaller robot and taking cover inside the bunker doorway.

"Get this door open!" yells Han when R2-D2 finally arrives. Then he turns to open fire on a couple of stormtroopers that have been shooting at them from behind a bush.

This time it's the troopers who have the better aim! R2 has barely plugged into the door's terminal when he's hit by a bright red blast. The little droid goes flying, head spinning and smoke pouring out of every interface.

"Oh, Artoo! Why did you have to be so brave?" moans C-3PO.

Side by side, Han and Leia return fire. Hard to see what's going on in the bushes but it looks like they got one. The other disappears.

Han looks at the control panel R2 opened. Inside there's a tangle of wires.

"I suppose I could try hotwiring this thing . . ." he says, though not with a lot of hope.

"I'll cover you," says Leia, taking another shot at the troopers' hiding spot.

CHAPTER SIXTY-FIVE

✦

IN WHICH TWO EWOKS AND A WOOKIEE ARE TOO MUCH FOR AN IMPERIAL WALKER

MEANWHILE, the Ewoks keep up the fight in the forest. They scored a major victory when they knocked over an AT-ST by rolling several logs at it. The giant metal thing actually slipped and fell. And I fear its pilot and copilot did not fare well once they crawled out of the wreckage.

However, the third AT-ST has been unstoppable, dodging traps and using its twin laser cannons with deadly accuracy. A whole tribe of Ewoks tried to bring it down by stretching out a vine for it to trip over. Instead, the little warriors were dragged along behind it until they let go.

But now they have a new plan . . . with a new ally. Chewbacca, they discover, is even better at climbing trees than they are.

Several Ewoks lure the AT-ST past a particular tree. Just as it passes underneath, Chewbacca—along with two rather reckless young Ewok hunters, Wunka and Widdle—drops down onto the roof of the big metal walker.

Wunka clambers to the very edge of the roof, leans over, and peeks through the windshield.

"Look!" yells the copilot.

"Get that thing off of there!" snarls the pilot.

The copilot lifts the hatch in the roof, but is immediately grabbed by Chewbacca and thrown to the forest floor.

Meanwhile, Widdle has already slipped through the hatch and stabbed the pilot through the . . . well, again, no need for the details here. The important thing to note is that when the pilot slumps forward over the controls, the walker stumbles and Chewie just barely hangs on to the hatch.

"NWWRGGK!" he fusses at Widdle.

Wunka hops down into the cockpit next and helpfully pulls at a control lever. The walker rears back and teeters wildly, almost falling backward. But Chewbacca has now dropped into the pilot's seat and he quickly gets the AT-ST balanced.*

Then, without wasting a second, he turns and heads back to the bunker, blasting troopers, bikers, and the fourth AT-ST as he goes.

"Mircheeewawaaaaaaa!" yells Wunka.

"MURRGGGGHHHRRRR!" agrees Chewbacca.

---

*An AT-ST is very, very difficult to control, but Chewbacca has driven and/or stolen just about every kind of vehicle at least once during his long, adventurous life.

CHAPTER SIXTY-SIX

✦

IN WHICH THE PRINCESS
SAVES THE DAY

BACK AT THE BUNKER, Han has stripped a few wires and now he touches the ends of two together. Sparks fly.

"I think I got it!"

He hooks another wire on and a loud click is heard.

"I got it!"

But instead of the bunker door opening, a second, heavier blast door slams down.

Leia turns to look and then—*KRRZAP!*—she's hit by a shot from a stormtrooper's blaster.

"Oh! Princess Leia!" cries C-3PO. "Are you all right?"

"It's not bad," says Leia, clutching her shoulder.

"Let's see," says Han, easing her to the ground and leaning down to look at the wound.

"Freeze!"

"Oh dear! Another stormtrooper! Where did *he* come from?"

"Don't move," barks the trooper.

Han looks at Leia. Is it all over?

Leia looks at Han with the tiniest smile. She reaches into her jacket and—with Han blocking the trooper's view—pulls out a pistol.

"I love you," says Han.

"I know," says Leia.

"Hands up! Stand up!" says the trooper.

Han straightens up and then quickly steps aside, giving Leia a clear shot at the trooper.

Pzzzap!

Han turns back to congratulate Leia and then freezes.

An AT-ST has stomped into the clearing, twin cannons pointed straight at him.

"Stay back," he whispers to Leia, but it's not

necessary. The walker's hatch pops open and there's Chewie, roaring in triumph!

"Mgrrruuuuuuu!"

"Chewie!" yells Han with relief.

Then he remembers Leia's injury. "Get down here! She's wounded!"

Then he remembers the mission: "No, wait! Stay there!"

He turns to Leia with a smile.

"I got an idea."

CHAPTER SIXTY-SEVEN

✦

IN WHICH LUKE GIVES IN
TO THE DARK SIDE

LUKE WATCHES the space battle as it wears on and on.

The two fleets are hopelessly tangled now. He can't be sure but he thinks Admiral Ackbar must have done this on purpose.

But why?

There can only be one answer: because the shield is still up.

That means that Han and Leia have failed. No, he dare not think of them.

He turns back to the battle and watches as a damaged rebel cruiser begins to come apart in a series of minor explosions. But with one last burst from its engines, it closes in on a Star Destroyer.

The cruiser silently explodes and the blast destroys most of the control tower of the Star Destroyer.

A victory of sorts. But not a happy one.

He tries to count the remaining rebel ships . . . not enough. He knows it's not enough.

"Your fleet has lost," croaks the Emperor. "And your friends on the Endor moon will not survive. There is no escape, my young apprentice. The Alliance will die . . . as will your friends."

Luke says nothing. But the Emperor seems to hear a response.

"Good, good. I can feel your anger! Take your weapon! I am defenseless. Strike me down with all your hatred and your journey to the dark side will be complete."

And Luke does! Or at least he tries to.

In a single motion, he whirls, reaches out with the Force for his lightsaber, fires it up, and swings it down to destroy the Emperor.

But just centimeters from the Emperor's face

a bright red blade blocks it. The Emperor never flinches.

Luke looks up. It's Vader . . . his own blazing red lightsaber crackling with energy.

And now the two must fight again.

Blades whirl and clash and spark. Luke crouches low, ready to either dodge or lunge. Vader stands tall and simply pushes forward, driving Luke backward with powerful swings.

But now Luke spins and changes the flow of the attack, surprising Vader who is just a little too slow to turn. Luke rushes in to bring down a mighty two-handed blow. Vader blocks it, but finds himself thrown off balance by the intensity of it. He steps back, not realizing that Luke had driven him to the edge of the stairs.

He falls and Luke is preparing to leap down after him when he hears the Emperor behind him.

"Good. Use your aggressive feelings, boy. Let the hate flow through you."

Again, the Emperor is telling the truth and

Luke knows it. He has won, but only by using the dark side of the Force. The hate *is* flowing through him and he is winning this battle against his father because of it.

Luke looks down at his father, clambering to his feet at the foot of the stairs. He had told Obi-Wan he couldn't kill his father . . . and yet he almost had.

He turns off his lightsaber and at the same time attempts to turn off the hate and anger.

Vader climbs the stairs, lightsaber still blazing and hate still flowing.

"Obi-Wan has taught you well."

"I will not fight you, Father," says Luke, staring into the black mask.

"You are unwise to lower your defenses!" booms Vader, suddenly swinging his light sword.

But Luke is not there. He is springing into the air, flipping backward, and landing high above Vader on a catwalk.

"Your thoughts betray you, Father. I feel the good in you . . . the conflict."

"There is no conflict!"

"You couldn't bring yourself to kill me before and I don't believe you'll destroy me now."

"You underestimate the power of the dark side! If you will not fight, then you will meet your destiny."

Vader flings his lightsaber. It slices through the catwalk and Luke falls to the ground, rolling away into the gloomy darkness of an unused area of the throne room.

The Emperor laughs and calls out, "Good, good," as if he were watching a show.

Vader puts out his hand and his lightsaber flies into it. He stalks into the darkness to find his son.

CHAPTER SIXTY-EIGHT

✪

IN WHICH HAN TRIES HIS IDEA, AND LET'S HOPE IT WORKS, BECAUSE THE REBELS ARE REALLY RUNNING OUT OF TIME

HAN'S IDEA, it turns out, is to use the AT-ST's video comlink to impersonate an Imperial again.

Climbing up to the cockpit, he swipes the jacket and helmet from the dead pilot, sits in the seat, and switches on the comlink.

"It's over, Commander. The rebels put up a fight, but they've been routed."

Han hears cheering coming through the comlink.*

---

*Some of the engineers and technicians had started to get a little nervous as the battle lasted longer than expected.

"They're fleeing into the woods," Han continues. "We need reinforcements to continue the pursuit."

"Very good," the commander replies, as if rebels are routed any and every time he's in charge. Now he turns to an underling and says, "Send a squad to help."

The squad, of course, has to open the door before they can rush out to help.

And when they open the door, they find themselves staring at an unrouted rebel strike team, a bunch of spear-waving Ewoks, a gun-toting princess, a triumphant Wookiee, and a smirking Han Solo.

Han, Chewie, and several rebels rush in, kick the crestfallen commander and his controllers out, place the explosives, and then make a run for it.

"Move! Move!" yells Han, running out of the bunker.

KRAKATHOOOOM!!!!!

There is a very big explosion and the control bunker blows up, triggering other explosions, which in turn cause the generator building to crumble, which results in the giant shield-casting dish slowly toppling over.

It is a strangely beautiful sight and those Ewoks who are nearby to see it will tell the story again and again for the rest of their lives.

But right now we don't have time to sit and watch, because this is the moment Ackbar and Lando and all the rebels have been waiting for.

High above the exploding generator, a display screen lights up on the rebel flagship and Ackbar leaps to his feet.

"The shield is down! Commence attack on the Death Star's main reactor!"

⬢

CHAPTER SIXTY-NINE

IN WHICH LUKE MEETS HIS DESTINY

"**Y**OU CANNOT HIDE FOREVER, LUKE."

"I will not fight you, Father," Luke calls from the darkness.

"Give yourself to the dark side," urges Vader. "It is the only way you can save your friends. Yes . . . your thoughts betray you. Your feelings for them are strong, especially for . . ."

Vader pauses. Luke grimaces. The Emperor rises from his throne to hear what Vader will say. This is unexpected.

"Sister! So . . . you have a twin sister. Obi-Wan was wise to hide her from me. But now his failure is complete. Your feelings have betrayed her, too. If you will not turn to the dark side, perhaps she will."

"Never!" screams Luke, launching himself out of the gloom, lightsaber blazing, fighting as he has never fought before.

He swings wildly, madly, using the dark side to move faster and strike harder. He has felt anger and hate before, but never this much fear . . . fear for his sister, Leia.

It is too much for Vader. He blocks attack after attack but is pushed back farther each time. Always fueled by hatred, he now gathers additional strength from fear . . . but it is not enough. Luke lands a blow on his arm, then one on his side.

The Sith Lord is forced backward until he reaches the bridge over the reactor shaft. Here he tries to strike back, but Luke knocks him down. He sprawls onto the bridge, lifting his lightsaber in a vain attempt to block whatever comes next. But Luke slashes with his saber, slicing Vader's arm off. The metal limb tumbles down into the shaft, taking the lightsaber with it.

And now Luke steps onto the bridge, pointing

the end of his fiery blade at Vader's throat.

The Emperor has come down the stairs to watch all this. It has gone just as he foresaw.

"Good! Your hate and your fear have made you more powerful. Now, fulfill your destiny and take your father's place at my side."

Take your father's place . . . The words ring in Luke's ears. He looks at his father and at his father's severed arm on the ground. But no, it's not a real arm. It's metal and wires, like . . . his own hand.

Take your father's place . . . Can this really be his destiny? To become more machine than man? To become the servant of the Emperor?

No, it can't be!

Take your father's place . . . He has come so close. One more swing of the lightsaber and his father will die and then, yes, he realizes . . . he would take his father's place. That is where this fight will take him. The only place it can take him. . . .

"Never!" he yells.

He throws his lightsaber aside.

He turns from his father to face the Emperor unarmed.

"I'll never turn to the dark side. You've failed, Your Highness. I am a Jedi, like my father before me."

"So be it, Jedi," hisses the Emperor, and blinding bolts of energy explode from his hands and instantly wrap themselves around Luke. He screams in agony, but stays on his feet, trying to use the Force to protect himself.

"If you will not be turned . . . you will be destroyed," cackles the Emperor, and as the hatred flows through him the Sith lightning intensifies and overcomes Luke.

He can feel the Emperor's thoughts screaming in his own mind, the swirling chaos of fresh anger and long-held hatreds, dark memories, and darker hopes. These hurt his mind even more than the dark lightning hurts his body.

"Young fool . . . only now at the end do you understand."

The Emperor is right. Luke had no idea that the dark side was *this* powerful, that the Force could be used *this* way. He does understand now and it is a terrible thing to understand.

Luke collapses under the onslaught, clutching at a railing to keep from being pushed into the reactor shaft behind him. But he can do nothing more. The storm of dark energy blots out his own thoughts and makes his body jerk and writhe.

"Your feeble skills are no match for the power of the dark side. You have paid the price for your lack of vision."

Luke forces his eyes open and sees that Vader is back on his feet and standing behind the Emperor.

"Father . . . please . . . help me . . ."

Vader looks on, his black mask giving no clue what he might be thinking.

The lightning eases for just a moment and the Emperor takes a last, thoughtful look at Luke. It has been pleasurable to cause this much pain, to unleash the horrors in his own head on another.

But now it is time to finally wipe out this threat to his empire. It was rather a small threat in the end, he thinks, hardly worth all the trouble he has taken.

"And now, young Skywalker . . . you will die."

The Emperor steps forward, bearing down on Luke and flinging his hands out in front of him. The lightning erupts again but stronger than before. And Luke's torment is worse than ever, worse than anything he's ever known.

And then, at last, Vader acts. Grabbing the Emperor with what is left of his arms, he lifts his master high in the air and lumbers toward the reactor shaft.

And now, with fear added to his anger and hatred, the Emperor turns a yet more powerful lightning attack on Vader. Countless blue bolts seethe across the black mask, burning into both metal and flesh. But though he must be feeling even more pain than Luke did, Vader staggers on.

When at last he reaches the open shaft he hurls the Emperor down into the reactor. It's a long,

long way down and the Emperor fires his lightning upward as he falls.

He might still have used his powers to save himself, but his hate is now so strong his only thought is to cause Vader more pain. So the lightning continues to flicker and flash even after the body is out of sight.

And then comes a great explosion when his body finally reaches the reactor and a poisonous wind races up the shaft, knocking Vader at last to the floor.

He comes close to falling into the shaft himself, but suddenly his son is there, pulling him back from the edge.

CHAPTER SEVENTY

✦

IN WHICH THE REBELS RAID THE DEATH STAR

OBVIOUSLY THERE are a lot of things on Luke's mind, but before he can even begin to sort it all out, the entire Death Star jolts wildly, nearly sending both him and his father into the pit.

He has no way of knowing what caused it, but he knows it must mean that the shield is down and the rebel attack is finally under way.

He wants the attack to succeed, of course, but he needs to get clear of it first . . . and take his father with him.

Battered and buffeted by first Vader and then the Emperor, Luke has little strength left, but he uses it all to drag his father across the bridge to the elevator. He searches his Jedi-sharpened memory for the floor of the docking bay where Vader's shuttle deposited him hours earlier.

When the elevator gets them to the right floor, the door opens to reveal chaos. Troopers, officers, underlings, and construction workers scramble in every direction. Some race to repair the damage, some race to defend the station, and some hang about so they'll be close to a ship when the call to evacuate comes.

They didn't know Luke was aboard, so now he passes as just another person in the way. And no one thinks for a second that the crumpled black burden he carries could possibly be the invincible Darth Vader. Vader, they are sure, is still stomping about somewhere protecting the Emperor.

In truth, Darth Vader is gone now. The body Luke eases gently to the floor is Anakin Skywalker.

"Luke, help me take this mask off," Anakin says, no longer booming.

"But you'll die."

"Nothing can stop that now. Just for once let me look on you with my own eyes."

It takes Luke a moment, but he soon discovers how the front of Vader's mask can be detached from the helmet and removed. When he does so, the sound of Vader's respirator, already ragged, stops.

And now Luke sees for himself the face of his father: scarred and battered into something barely human.

And now Anakin sees his son's face: a handsome face, creased with concern and, yes, bearing its own battle scars.

But at last Anakin sees him not as a Jedi or a warrior or a threat or a mistake, but as his son . . . and Padmé's son.

And Anakin smiles. Not a smile like the Emperor's. Or a crazed grin like Darth Maul's. Not even a smirk like Anakin might have shown Ahsoka back in his Jedi days.

But a real smile.

The smile that only Padmé ever saw.

"Now . . . go, my son," Anakin struggles to say. "Leave me."

"No. You're coming with me. I can't leave you here! I've got to save you!"

"You already have, Luke. You were right. You were right about me. Tell your sister . . . you were right."

"Father . . . I won't leave you."

And then another great jolt! Luke looks up to see cargo crates spilling, troopers running, and an officer barking orders that no one stops to listen to.

When he looks back down, his father is dead. But Luke keeps his promise. He will not leave his father. He stumbles toward the distant shuttle, staggering under the weight of this giant half-metal man who wrought so much evil.

Leave him there, you want to shout to Luke. He's the bad guy! The villain! Just leave him and get out of there before the whole Death Star blows up!*

---

*You do have a point about the whole thing being about ready to explode.

I can't blame you for that, reader, but think of this:

In the end, Anakin did what no Jedi—not Luke, not Obi-Wan, not even Yoda—could do.

In killing his master—the mighty Sith Lord Darth Sidious, known to the galaxy as Emperor Palpatine—Anakin fulfilled his destiny and restored balance to the Force. And so, though the galaxy will not honor him . . . Luke will.

CHAPTER SEVENTY-ONE

· ✦ ·

IN WHICH THE WHOLE
THING EXPLODES

HREE X-WINGS and the *Millennium Falcon* scorch across the surface of the Death Star toward a gap in the incomplete side of the giant space station.

"I'm going in!" calls Wedge. He and his wingmen suddenly drop into the hole in the side of the space station. The *Falcon* is maneuverable, but not *that* maneuverable. Lando has to take it up into a tight backflip and then dive straight down into the unfinished innards of the Death Star.

"Here goes nothing," he says, but that's just space jockey talk. He's got his foot on the throttle and Nien Nunb's got his finger on the trigger. They know that this is *something*.

Though unfinished, this Death Star was going to have some improvements over the last one. You may recall that a ventilation shaft that led straight to the main reactor doomed that one. The ventilation shafts are still there—we just saw the Emperor fall down one, after all—but this time Jerjerrod made sure the exhaust ports were very, very, very heavily armored. In the plans, at least.

And, had the Emperor allowed Jerjerrod more time—not to mention more money and more workers—the whole thing would have been shut up tight.*

But an unfinished Death Star was part of the bait for the Emperor's trap . . . and now it's providing just enough room for the fighters and the *Falcon* to slip through a crack in the armor and shoot straight for the heart of the space station, the reactor core.

Unfortunately, there's also enough space for TIE fighters to slip in behind them.

"Now lock on to the strongest power source,"

---

*And Jerjerrod has the paperwork to prove it!

Lando tells Nien Nunb. "It should be the power generator."

"Form up and stay tight," Wedge tells his wing-men. "We could run out of space real fast."

Unfortunately, there's no straight shot this time. This shaft was never finished and is half clogged with huge cables, construction equipment, and scaffolding. Lando has to spin the *Falcon* this way and that to squeeze through.

The compact TIEs are better suited for this space. They've caught up with the rebels and rake them with cannon fire.

BZZZZRAK!

One of them hits an X-wing. The pilot struggles to regain control but the tunnel's just too tight! The X-wing spins into a wall and explodes, almost taking the *Falcon* out with it.

"Deh-te'ill DOU!" yells Nien Nunb.

"Agreed," calls back Lando. "Maybe this will do it." He points ahead to a large gap in the tunnel, where one wall is still incomplete.

Lando leans toward the comlink: "Wedge, stay with me. The rest of you split up and head back to the surface and see if you can take some of those TIE fighters with you."

"Copy, Gold Leader."

Four X-wings peel off and shoot through the gap. Two TIEs follow them, but four remain locked on to Lando and Wedge.

One of these scores a direct hit on the *Falcon*.

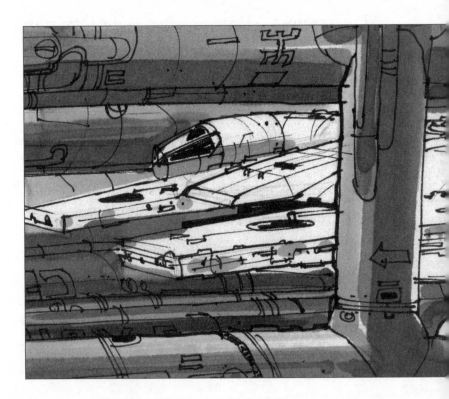

The deflector shield holds, but the impact sends the ship into a tailspin just as the tunnel up ahead is half blocked.

Lando manages to regain control and shoots through the narrowing gap, but not without slamming the *Falcon*'s topside into a wall. There's an awful lurch as various parts of the *Falcon* are ripped away, but the hull holds and the ship just keeps on going.

"That was *too* close," mutters Lando.

"Mu–the gate–oh . . ."

Now the tunnel opens up into a cavernous space with a glowing reactor at its center. They see Wedge's X-wing hurtling toward it.

"Lor–ac!! Lor–ac!!" yells Nien Nunb!

"All right! Wedge, go for the power regulator on the side tower."

"Copy, Gold Leader. . . . I'm already on my way out," comes the response.

Wedge fires his torpedoes and then peels away. They explode into a huge metal structure perched on the side of the reactor.

The *Falcon* keeps straight ahead until it's almost swallowed by the glowing mass at the center. Nien Nunb fires directly into it and then Lando hauls on the wheel to just barely avoid the reactor and follow Wedge back to the surface.

But behind them the reactor is exploding. Will they get out in time?

Out in the relative safety of the space battle,

Ackbar has heard Wedge and orders, "Move the fleet away from the Death Star."

A feeling of triumph and, yes, disbelief grows inside Ackbar. After all these years of fighting, the Empire is about to be destroyed.

But will the *Falcon* be destroyed with it?

Unnoticed by either the panicking Imperials or the triumphing rebels, Darth Vader's shuttle slips out of a docking bay and heads for the forest moon, carrying Luke and what remains of Anakin Skywalker.

Yes, good, we figured Luke would get out in time. But what about the *Falcon*?

Lando fires the afterburners and the *Falcon* screams through another tunnel, clipping corners and smashing through anything that looks smash-throughable.

Yes, yes . . . we know the *Falcon*'s fast. But is it faster than the explosion of the largest reactor the galaxy's ever seen?

No . . . it's not.

For a moment it looks like they might outrun the explosion. But just as Lando and Nien Nunb see starlight at the end of the tunnel, it catches up with them, consumes them, engulfs them in a white-hot fireball.

The Death Star has gone supernova. Everything melts or burns or detonates or sometimes all three.

Well, not quite everything, reader, not quite everything . . .

The *Millennium Falcon* is a very special ship. It's not

just her speed. Solo and Chewie made some special modifications themselves, remember.

So . . .

From out of the firecloud, the *Falcon* bursts into open space!

"YAHOOOOOOOO!" shouts Lando.

"Haha haha hahahaha," laughs Nien Nunb, consumed by joy.

It is a joy that will spread and grow as the news goes out: the galaxy is free again.

CHAPTER SEVENTY-TWO

✦

IN WHICH THE NEWS
REACHES ENDOR

N THE FOREST, not far from the bunker, Han
Solo is bandaging the blaster wound on Leia's
shoulder. It's worse than she admitted earlier,
but this will do until a medical droid can take
care of it.

Suddenly, the Ewoks are shouting. Then the
strike team is whooping. Then Chewbacca is roaring. And C-3PO is babbling.

The early evening sky gets bright. Han and Leia
shield their eyes and look up.

High in the sky, the metal moon is silently coming undone.

Their mission is a success! The whole rebellion
is a success!

But Han doesn't join in the cheering. He turns to Leia.

"I'm sure Luke wasn't on that thing when it blew."

"He wasn't. I can feel it."

"You love him, don't you?" Han asks.

Leia smiles. "Yes."

"All right. I understand. Fine," says Han. "When he comes back, I won't get in the way."

Leia's smile widens.

"Oh. No, it's not like that at all. He's my brother."

"Oh," says Han, then pauses to think what this means. And then pauses a little longer to think what it all means. "Oh!"

And they kiss. And it is such a meaningful kiss, such a passionate kiss, that I'm relieved to say that it is soon interrupted by Wicket hurling himself at them with an ecstatic *"Meeeercheeewawaaaa!!!!"*

CHAPTER SEVENTY-THREE

✪

IN WHICH TWO FIRES
BURN ON ENDOR

LUKE LANDS THE SHUTTLE some distance from his friends. Though exhausted, he asks no one's help in building a funeral pyre for his father. To all the rest of the galaxy, the sight of Vader's helmet consumed by fire would be cause for rejoicing. Another of the joys of victory.

But to Luke alone, it is something different.

No, that is not correct. He is not alone.

Watching from the edge of the firelight are three who understand. Glowing, flickering, just barely there. But they are there.

Obi-Wan Kenobi. Yoda. And Anakin.

All three are at peace now that balance has returned to the Force, and they smile at Luke, pleased to know that, despite the best efforts of the Emperor, the Jedi have returned.

Each in turn thinks to warn Luke about the future. For each has seen that there is yet much danger ahead for Luke and more darkness to overcome.

But each in turn decides not to burden Luke with this now. He has earned this peace, this time of balance for the galaxy . . . let him enjoy it for as long as it lasts.

Luke sees them, feels their approval and their sense of peace, and now at last he begins to feel the joy that his friends are feeling.

As the ghosts of the three Jedi fade into the night, Luke turns away from the smoldering remains of the funeral pyre and moves toward the Ewoks' victory bonfire to join his friends.

CHAPTER SEVENTY-FOUR

✦

IN WHICH WE, TOO, JOIN THE PARTY BEFORE SAYING GOOD-BYE TO OUR HEROES

T HERE ARE celebrations all across the galaxy. The claws of Palpatine have finally released their grip and free people pour into the streets of Coruscant, the plazas of Naboo, and the corridors of Cloud City.*

They cheer for the end of a war and the end of the Empire—and some, like Mon Mothma, are already cheering the start of a new Republic.

But nowhere is the celebration equal to that on the forest moon of Endor, where the joy of freedom

---

*And, yes, even in the cantinas of Mos Eisley.

is mixed with the exultation of a battle won against impossible odds.

"Yub nub!" chant the Ewoks, whooping, dancing, drumming, drinking, and feasting.*

There's Wicket, who got his wish for adventure. And old Chief Chirpa, who had thought his adventures were behind him.

There's Romba, who won justice for his lost village. And Teebo and Paploo and Asha and many more who had flung themselves into an unwinnable battle and won.

Many Ewoks died and they will be mourned tomorrow and for many, many days after. But tonight the Ewoks burst with the thrill of gaining what they have all fought for:

"YUB NUB!"

They repeat this phrase again and again. *"Yub nub! Yub nub!"* They can't stop, and why should they?

---

*Perhaps, reader, it would be better not to ask where all this fresh meat came from.

It's a chant; it's a song; it's a prayer of thanks to their golden god, C-3PO.

C-3PO, in fact, is the only one who knows that it means "freedom," but he can't find anyone to tell, except R2, who has been rebooted after his misadventure at the bunker and is chirping and whistling happily.

All the rebels give a cheer as Lando, Nien Nunb, and Wedge come running in. Han and Chewie rush over to embrace Lando . . . and ask about the *Falcon*.

"Not a scratch," lies Lando, with a big smile.

And then Luke arrives at last. Everyone crowds around. There are so many questions. Is Vader really dead? The Emperor, too?

Yes, yes, but he must find Leia, his sister, the only one who knows or can even begin to understand what has just happened. And soon he does and they embrace, first with relief, then joy, then sadness—the great sadness of their mother and father.

But the sorrow cannot last long . . . not with

the whole galaxy celebrating, and certainly not with their friends—Ewoks and droids and rebels and a scoundrel and a Wookiee—all calling to them.

So they turn to join the celebration, such a celebration as was never had before and will never be had again.

Shall we join them, reader? Yes, let's dance and laugh and whoop and yell *"yub nub"* until the sun comes up over the forest.

AUTHOR BIOGRAPHY

T**OM ANGLEBERGER**, author of the *New York Times* best-selling Origami Yoda series, has been a *Star Wars* fan and collector since 1977. Growing up before the dawn of the VCR, Tom listened to *Star Wars* again and again on cassette tape. His first action figure was C-3PO and his most recent (very recent) was a sandtrooper. He lives in Virginia with his wife, author and illustrator Cece Bell.